THE MIRACLE OF LOVE

When Holly's much longed-for promotion goes to handsome outsider Joel Richards, she has reason to suspect that something mysterious is going on. This is confirmed when Joel replaces the store's regular Santa Claus with yet another outsider and there follows a string of Christmas burglaries. With her career in jeopardy and the interests of her young clients at heart, Holly decides to investigate and ends up being more involved with her new boss than she ever imagined possible.

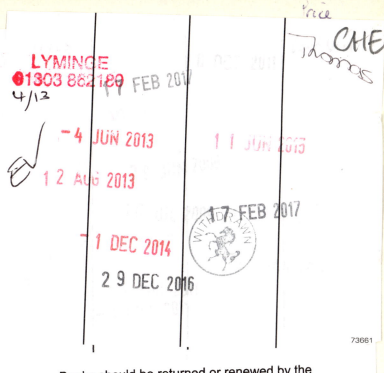

Awarded for excellence

Kent
County
Council

JUNE GADSBY

---◆---

THE
MIRACLE
OF LOVE

Complete and Unabridged

LINFORD
Leicester

First published in Great Britain in 2004

First Linford Edition
published 2005

British Library CIP Data

Gadsby, June
    The miracle of love.—Large print ed.—
Linford romance library
    1. Romantic suspense novels
    2. Large type books
    I. Title
    823.9'2 [F]

    ISBN 1–84617–030–3

Published by
F. A. Thorpe (Publishing)
Anstey, Leicestershire

Set by Words & Graphics Ltd.
Anstey, Leicestershire
Printed and bound in Great Britain by
T. J. International Ltd., Padstow, Cornwall

This book is printed on acid-free paper

1

'Well, today's the day,' Holly told herself as she sailed merrily into work. In her mind she could see nothing but blue skies and a future that was like the pot of gold at the end of her own personal rainbow. Her career was in the bag.

She was aware of every pair of eyes in the store watching her — bright eyes, friendly eyes, and maybe some jealous ones.

No-one, least of all Holly, expected the bombshell of bad news that was about to burst.

Ever since leaving secretarial college, Holly had worked for The Playpen. A toyshop with a difference, it had been her second home when she was a young child and all she ever wanted to do was work there.

The dream had easily been realised.

She became junior this, assistant that, and now, at the age of twenty-eight, she was proud of her Assistant Manager status.

Everybody knew that once Mr Matthews retired, in about ten years, the post of Branch Manager would automatically become hers. She didn't mind waiting. It would be worth it, in the end.

No-one, of course, expected poor old Arnold Matthews to fall ill. All those months that he was in and out of hospital, Holly had coped. Everybody remarked on how well she had done. Her final promotion was in the offing much sooner than expected and it was just a matter of time before the news would be made official.

However, red tape being what it was, when Arnold took early retirement because of ill-health, Holly had to go through the normal, by-the-book rig-marole of applying for the now vacant managerial post. And, of course, the job had to be advertised externally as well as internally.

And since she was the only internal candidate everyone knew that it was going to be game, set and match — to Holly Duncan.

'Good luck, Holly! You deserve it, lass.'

She heard the voices of encouragement float out to her.

'Not that you'll need it, mind!'

Of course she didn't need luck. She had proved to her employers time and time again that she could run the shop blindfold. Even Arnold Matthews had given her a strong letter of recommendation as his successor. Absolutely nothing could stand in her way.

But nothing, it seems, is ever one hundred per cent sure. The grey head and plain face of Miss Loach, the personnel officer, peered at Holly through the half-glazed widows of her office.

Her small, beady eyes, looking more anxious than usual, followed Holly's every step as she strode confidently up the corridor to the manager's office, which she had occupied for the last eighteen months.

'Miss Duncan! A word, if you please.'

There was a suppressed titter of laughter and one or two hastily muttered remarks behind hands. Some of the staff gave Holly the thumbs up sign, winking at her with knowing smiles.

'Good morning, Miss Loach. Isn't it a beautiful day!'

Miss Loach never wasted time on small talk.

'I'm terribly sorry to disappoint you, Miss Duncan,' she said without preamble.

'Why? What's happened?'

Already, Holly's heart began to tumble from that euphoric cloud nine.

The personnel officer looked uncomfortable and hugged her big, chunky home-knit cardigan to her as if a sudden chill had struck her. She tried to look friendly, which wasn't easy, for she was naturally dour.

'The interviewing committee has asked me to break the news to you, though, of course, you will be notified officially in writing. The fact is . . . '

'I didn't get the job?' Holly gulped and almost choked on it.

The supervisor closed her eyes, shutting them tightly, then opened them and gazed at the ceiling.

'I'm afraid not.'

Holly staggered to a chair and sat down heavily. All that laughing and cajoling by everyone who, like her, firmly believed that the interview was just a matter of protocol! How humiliating it was going to be, having to face them all now.

'What did I do wrong?' she asked, so sure in herself that the interview had gone well.

'Ah! No, there was nothing — nothing like that.'

The woman dragged her eyes from the ceiling and searched the room, hunting frantically for some item upon which she could anchor her gaze.

'Everyone was agreed that you had all the merits of a good branch manager, but . . . '

'But they didn't want me? Why was that, Miss Loach?'

Holly stopped herself short of ranting and raving. After all, she had worked and slaved for years with this one career move in mind.

'They felt that perhaps you were not quite experienced enough . . . ' Miss Loach spread her hands. 'I'm sorry, my dear, but they've given the job to another candidate — a Mr Joel Richards from London.'

'From London!'

'I know we usually appoint from existing staff or local candidates, if we can at all do so, but . . . ' Again there was the spread of hands and a slight shrug of her painfully thin shoulders. 'Mr Richards came with a lot of experience and excellent references — which you also have, Miss Duncan. Please don't get me wrong, but . . . '

But! That tiny word that could make

or break just about anything. Miss Loach didn't have to say any more. Holly had seen this Mr Joel Richards who had robbed her of her future career — tall, dark, suave and self-assured, oh, yes, and tremendously handsome. And the appointing committee consisted largely of females, at least two of them, she had heard, from the large London branch where Mr Richards worked. Enough said.

Holly remembered the way Joel Richards had looked at her as they waited together outside the interview room three days ago.

His dark eyes, so dazzling when he smiled, had made her shudder with an emotion she had yet to work out. He had charm, too, and a velvety voice to die for. No wonder they were appointing him.

He had wished her good luck as she went into the interview room before him and he seemed so genuine that Holly had thought he probably meant it. He even asked how it went when she came out, looking, she was sure, all glassy-eyed and pink cheeked like a schoolgirl applying for her first job.

On Joel Richards' first day as manager of The Playpen, there was an almost palpable silence among the staff.

Mostly, it was because they sensed Holly's disappointment and sympathised. But there was a lot of breath being held when he walked in and introduced himself.

Not many shop managers looked quite as good as he did, she admitted grudgingly, but she was blinded by her disillusionment and — yes, OK, her jealousy. She was all set not to like Mr Joel Richards, no matter what.

⋆   ⋆   ⋆

'This is really embarrassing,' he said from the open door of Holly's, or now, their office. 'I gather you were expected to be the next branch manager and I sort of whipped the job out from under your feet.'

'Don't worry,' she told him, forcing a very insincere smile that froze hard on her lips. 'I have big feet and very broad shoulders. I suppose this is your desk now. Just give me a few minutes to clear my stuff.'

Holly saw him start to protest, but then he looked towards the other desk that was tucked in the corner. It was small and insignificant and totally inadequate for his needs. He was a big man. It would be almost impossible for him to fit physically into that space.

'That's very kind of you. There's no hurry,' he said quickly.

Holly called one of the girls from the shop floor and instructed her to take Mr Richards off and introduce him to the rest of the staff. She knew she should have done the honours herself, and she felt badly about that deep inside.

However, her stubborn horns were making themselves felt and she couldn't backtrack now. Let him see that he has created an unnecessary situation here, she thought meanly. This reaction wasn't at all like her, so she immediately began to feel guilty all over again.

By the time he came back, she had transferred herself and her belongings to the second-class desk and was sitting there calmly and trying not to look as demolished as she felt.

'It's quite a shop you have here,' he said with a winsome smile.

It might have charmed her socks off had they met socially, though she was never fortunate enough to come across this kind of man in her modest social encounters. She tended to meet dull laboratory assistants or librarians who all wore the uniform of the ordinary man — the sloppy sweater and the jeans.

Joel Richards looked as if he had muscles, but he wasn't flaunting them. They were smartly disguised beneath a finely-tailored Armani suit.

'The Playpen? Well, I like it,' she said and shuffled papers around unnecessarily in order to look busy. 'I've known it since I was about five.'

'Lucky you,' he said with an even broader smile that turned into a mischievous grin.

This unearthed a flurry of butterflies in Holly's stomach, but she thought that it was probably because she was in a state of nervous anxiety and hadn't eaten breakfast.

'We pride ourselves on being different,' she rabbited on, wishing she could just sink into some dim, forlorn corner and be ignored.

'I like the concept of the crèche and, even better, a parents' corner. It's great that hassled mothers can flop and chat over a cup of coffee and a sticky bun.'

One side of Holly's mouth stretched up into a wry smile. Both the crèche and the parents' corner had been her original idea two years after joining the firm. And the sticky buns were wicked, as she knew to her calorific peril.

Holly shifted uncomfortably in her seat as she caught him appraising her from head to foot, unashamedly taking in every contour. And she had contours, much to her shame, which overstepped the mark, mainly because of the aforementioned sticky buns and regular sneaky chocolate bars by way of consolation for whatever was lacking in her life.

He had dimples when he smiled, long, deep indentations beneath high cheekbones. The Tom Selleck type, only younger.

2

As it happened, there weren't any trans-fers available at that particular time, so they came up with a new position instead. At least, Holly liked to think that it had been created for her, but the new job didn't come with any guarantees.

'Customer Relations Officer?'

Joel's eyebrows creased, then unfolded like ravens' wings.

'It's time The Playpen had somebody in charge of customer needs and complaints and you have shown a lot of potential in that direction. Don't turn it down, Holly. The job's tailor-made for you.'

'Where will I be based?'

He chewed on his mouth and gave her a lop-sided smile that made her heart sink like a stone, mainly because she knew exactly what he was going to tell her.

'You'll be based here, since this is the senior branch. Most of the time, customers bring their complaints to us anyway. Later on, if we expand, you could transfer to another branch.'

'I see. And my office? There will be an office?'

Holly fixed him with a challenging stare and saw him flinch.

'Ah, yes . . . ' He dug his hands into his jacket pockets and paced the floor in front of her before leaning over her desk, his face a little too close to hers for comfort. 'For the moment, Holly, I'm afraid you'll still be sharing with me, until they can renovate the old storeroom and then you can have an office all to yourself.'

'I see.'

He gave a small shrug, but his eyes were wary.

'Of course, the decision is entirely in your own hands. It's a new post with a lot of potential. I'd think about it before turning it down. That is, if you are thinking of turning it down, which I hope you are not. We really do need a good CRO, especially since Christmas is rushing up on us.'

Christmas. He had said the magic word. Had it been midsummer, Holly might have told him what to do with his job, but here they were in November already and she hadn't missed a Christmas at The Playpen in more years than she cared to remember.

She swallowed hard and met his gaze, which wasn't easy because it always did something to her insides that made her feel much too vulnerable. Why her resentment of this dark, good-looking charmer should shoot her full of electrical charges she would never know, but every time she thought about him millions of butterflies exploded into erratic life in her stomach. It was ridiculous. She didn't even like him.

'When will they start work on the storeroom?'

He contemplated the question, mulling it over in his mind.

'I can't give you an exact date, of

15

course, but it's scheduled for mid-January, February at the latest, after the stocktaking.'

It seemed a long time to wait for a bit of independent space and privacy.

'I see.'

'Holly, I do wish you would stop saying 'I see' like that. It really isn't my fault, you know, whatever it is that's annoying you.'

'Of course I know it isn't your fault. What a ridiculous idea. Anyway, there's nothing annoying me.'

'I'm glad to hear it. Do you think we can manage to be friends now, then?'

'Don't be silly. Of course.'

She was trying desperately to be rational. Her career depended on it.

He smiled and she melted just a little bit around the frozen wastes of her brittle veneer. They stood there, staring stupidly at one another, until a sudden waling from an infant broke the spell.

'It looks like I'm already needed in my new capacity,' Holly said ruefully and went off to see if she could reunite the first ubiquitous lost child of the day with its mother.

★   ★   ★

A few days later Holly had a new, larger desk, her own computer and a badge with her name and rank emblazoned on it. She was even given a filing cabinet and a mobile phone on which the sales assistants could alert her of impending, or ongoing, disasters in the store and request her presence if need be.

It was pretty much the kind of work she had been doing as assistant manager, but more intensely specified. She was kept busy from morning till night, almost as if the creation of the new post had also created the necessity for it.

Holly was just packing up to leave one evening when Miss Loach knocked and entered. Joel was away on business, attending a toy fair and a managers' conference, so she had been on her own in the office for a while. It had been a relief to know that he was going to be absent, but a surprise to find that she actually missed his heavy presence.

'Miss Duncan — sorry to bother you so late, but I've just had a phone call from Mr Richards.'

'Oh?' Holly frowned at the personnel officer, wondering what Joel was doing phoning her so late on a Friday afternoon.

'It seems he isn't gong to be back this evening after all. Some personal crisis at home — his family lives in London, as you know . . . '

Yes, Holly did know that, though she knew precious little of his private life, since he never talked about it and it wasn't her style to probe.

'I don't understand, Miss Loach. Why are you telling me this?'

She went on clearing her desk and locking away a small collection of lost and found items that had been dropped or discarded by the junior clientele who might eventually make their way back to the store to reclaim them.

'Because, my dear, we were supposed to have the Santa Claus interviews tomorrow morning and there isn't time to reschedule.'

Holly's frown deepened. She knew all about these mythical Santa Claus interviews, just as in her case, they were required to advertise the job externally.

There were usually numerous applicants who mainly wanted to come inside out of the cold and fill themselves with free food and drink. Their exuberance had little to do with the donning of a red suit and hat trimmed with while fluffy pompoms.

However, in reality, the shop had only ever employed one Santa Claus in the last thirty years, Fred Barnstable. He was naturally big, bonnie and booming. The kids loved him. Even Holly had sat on his knee when she was three and listed her wants for Christmas morning.

She stared at Miss Loach and waited. They had been going through the same old red tape interview for years. She couldn't see why this year should present a particular problem, unless Joel felt honour bound to be present.

'We won't be using Fred Barnstable this year,' Miss Loach said eventually, then followed it up quickly with, 'It's Mr Richards' decision.'

'What! But how can we not use Fred? He's part of the firm — part of The Playpen family.'

Miss Loach looked worried.

'I know that, but Mr Richards has given me strict instructions . . . ' She coughed discreetly behind her hand. '. . . and a shortlist of one, a certain Mr Charles Smith. Oh, there'll be others to interview, but we're to appoint this — um — Mr Smith. And you are to be on the interview panel to make it look official.'

Holly was stunned. The nerve of the man.

'Surely there's a law against this kind of thing — what's it called — nepotism?'

Miss Loach shook her head.

'I've already complained to the MD and he practically bit my head off. We're to follow Mr Richards' instructions to the letter. I just don't know how I'm going to break the news to Fred.'

Fred was the only person Holly had ever heard Miss Loach call by his first name. She obviously had a bit of a soft spot for him that went back a long way, but then they all had.

★　★　★

Holly went home to her cold little flat and stewed over Joel Richards. The business over the shop Santa Claus was so blatantly unethical and unfair. What made this Charles Smith character so special that poor Fred was left out in the cold, she wondered.

When she saw the man in question Holly wondered about it even more so. Mr Smith did not exactly fit the Santa Claus criteria, despite the genuine beard and that was grey rather than white.

Still, orders were orders and nobody dared show displeasure in front of this rather soft-spoken, unassuming old man whose tired blue eyes lit up at being congratulated on his success.

'Well, I never,' he said to Holly as she walked out of the store with him, hoping she could find a red suit with snowy white trim small enough by Wednesday. 'When Joel told me to apply for this job, I must say I didn't think I would get it. It just goes to show, doesn't it?'

Holly blinked at him, wondering what exactly it did go to show, except they were falling over backward to employ a stranger and discarding the regular and beloved Fred Barnstable.

'So, you know Mr Richards?' she prompted and saw him tense up slightly.

'Oh, I wouldn't say I know him — not really.' He turned and grasped Holly's hand warmly. 'Thank you, my dear. Now, don't you worry. I won't let you down. Being Santa Claus is something of a secret ambition. It's such an achievement to get there at last.'

Even if you got there by walking over someone else, Holly thought uncharitably, and wondered what it was about the man that she could not quite trust. He was impeccably dressed and well spoken. Maybe that was it. He didn't look the type of person who needed a job.

Mr Smith gave a small salute and Holly watched him walk away slowly, losing himself in the throng of Saturday shoppers.

There was nothing about him to make her suspicious, but she couldn't ignore that nagging feeling deep down inside. She made a mental note to have strong words with Joel Richards when he got back from whatever family crisis he was attending. He was going to find out just exactly what she thought of him and his unethical behaviour.

Just you wait, Mr Joel Richards, Holly told the image of him that she had in her head. You'll find I'm not somebody you can cross and get away with it. And if there's some kind of funny business going on, I'm going to get right to the bottom of it, you mark my words.

Holly virtually stormed into the personnel officer's room just as the woman was leaving, so she was hardly pleased to see her.

'Oh, Miss Duncan, if it's not urgent can it wait until Monday?'

'No, I'm afraid it can't, Miss Loach.'

Holly was amazed at her own bravado, but anger was giving her the courage to go on regardless.

'Having Mr Richards appointed as branch manager, when everyone expected me to get the job, was bad enough. Now, he decides that Fred Barnstable is going to be replaced by some unknown person by the name of Charles Smith who, to my knowledge, has never done this kind of work before. Is there some new company policy that I should know about?'

'Oh, dear!' Miss Loach seemed to deflate before her like an old-fashioned pair of bellows. 'I really can't discuss the matter with you, my dear. You see, it's all rather confidential. I do understand how you feel, believe me, but I'm sworn to secrecy.'

'Secrecy! Just what kind of secrecy are you talking about, Miss Loach? Who exactly is Joel Richards? And why should he be giving Fred's job to some mysterious stranger who looks as if he could afford to buy the whole store?'

Miss Loach closed her eyes and shook her head.

'I can't tell you, and please — Holly — please don't go asking questions. It could make a difficult situation more difficult. Much more difficult, I assure you.'

She had called Holly by her first name. It sort of put her on the same level as Fred Barnstable. Holly wasn't at all sure that it was a good sign.

'Who else knows about this — this secret?'

Miss Loach gave a little gasp and put her hand in front of her mouth.

'Oh, dear! I really should not have mentioned it. Please, Holly, just forget everything I said. It's for the best, believe me.'

★   ★   ★

Miss Loach had been so flustered by Holly's questioning that she had forgotten to lock her office later that day. Feeling wicked and a touch excited, Holly pulled out the drawer in the filing cabinet that housed the staff records.

Miss Loach was still to be persuaded to trust her computer and kept a printout of everything — just in case.

First, Holly pulled out Joel Richards' file, then Charles Smith's. They were new and there was a striking similarity between them. The contents of both had been removed, or had never been there. The files were completely empty.

She hunted through the papers on

Miss Loach's desk, thinking that she might have been lax that day and not filed away the records in question in their appropriate folders. Nothing.

The mystery of the two men was already deepening in Holly's mind and she had a growing premonition that she was getting involved in some disreputable business that she would have been happier without.

*　　*　　*

Later that day, as she walked into the underground carpark where she garaged her car during the week, Holly had the uncanny feeling that the place wasn't as deserted as it appeared. Most of the cars had gone and an eerie silence pervaded the dark, exhaust-fume filled atmosphere.

Twice, she stopped, thinking she heard something. A cough, a scrape of a shoe on the gritty road surface. Each time, she tried to hold her breath, breathing through her open mouth and seeing clouds of frozen vapour rise before her.

By the time a large, dark figure stepped out of the shadows and grabbed her arm, she was more than ready to scream.

'Holly!'

Holly was halfway to fainting with fright when she recognised the bulky figure of Fred Barnstable. His eyes were rheumier than ever and his bulbous nose more rosy than she had ever seen it.

'Fred! Goodness, you scared the living daylights out of me,' Holly complained breathlessly. 'What on earth are you doing lurking in here like this?'

'I was just waiting for you,' he told her, glancing briefly to left and to right. ''Ere, Holly, what's going on back there? You know I'm always The Playpen Santa Claus. Why are they not giving me the job this year? Can you tell me that? I mean, what are my children going to think when some other geezer shows up in my place?

They'll lose all faith in me.'

'I'm sorry, Fred.' Holly grimaced and tried to stop her heart from beating a loud tattoo against her rib cage. 'I have no idea what's happening. It was some kind of decision at the top, a change of policy.'

'Fishy business, if you ask me.' He pulled something out of his pocket and thrust it at her. 'Speaking of which, here you are. Take a look at this, then.'

Holly looked. It was an envelope and inside it there was a wad of bank notes.

'Where did you get this, Fred?'

'It was handed to me by Miss Loach when she told me that somebody else was going to be me this year. She said it was compensation and I hadn't to say nuthin' to nobody. But, Holly, love, there's more money there than I ever earned before as Santa Claus. What does it all mean, that's what I want to know?'

'Me, too, Fred,' she told him, handing him back the money. 'The powers-that-be obviously feel badly enough to want you to have a merry Christmas on them.'

'I dunno, Holly. It smells a bit, don't it? I mean, I never was one to be dishonest and this here money — it gives me a funny feeling inside. I didn't earn it, did I? It's like they're paying me off — you know — like in them Mafia films.'

Holly laughed, but at the same time she felt a cold trickle of fear wend its way slowly up and down her rigid spine.

3

'Holly, for goodness sake, calm down!' Her mother's voice sang at her through the telephone. Holly had rung to thank her for her Christmas card. It got earlier each year.

She would have been devastated to learn that anyone got their seasonal greeting in before she did. It was also, Holly was sure, a way of saying that she was not going to be available at Christmas.

Holly's reason for being irate was that she had just finished telling her mother about Joel and his peculiar methods of hiring staff.

'I detest nepotism!'

'Oh, come on, Holly! It's the season of goodwill and all that.'

Her mother continued to pour oil on troubled waters, but it wasn't having any helpful effect.

'Yes, I know, but all the same, Mum . . . '

'You're obviously upset by not getting the job of your dreams, but it's not life-threatening you know. Anyway, something else will turn up and you'll wonder what all the fuss was about.'

'Nobody's making a fuss!' Holly spoke a little more sharply than she should have.

'That's funny. I thought you were.'

'Well, I'm not. Goodness, Mum, Joel Richards isn't worth it.'

'Oh?'

'No. He comes over all good looks and charm and has every female in the store worshiping him — well, except me, that is. Fortunately, I can see right through men like that.'

'Can you, dear?'

'You'll not see me getting caught out again, I can assure you.'

'Yes, dear — I mean, no — oh! Did I tell you that your stepfather and I are going to Barbados for Christmas?'

Holly sighed.

'No, I don't think you did.'

'Well, it's just not the same any more staying at home,' her mother said with a deep sigh. 'Christmas needs children to give it that cosy, traditional feel. The old-fashioned family unit, you know.'

'Yes, I know,' Holly responded, hoping her mother wasn't going to go on at her again for not providing her with grandchildren before now.

'Have you got any plans yet? I mean, if you're really going to be alone, you must say. I'm sure we could organise another seat on the plane, though come to think of it the hotel is probably fully booked by now.'

'Don't worry about me, Mum,' Holly said. 'You know how I hate playing gooseberry to you and Nigel.'

'I knew you'd understand, dear. It's a bit of a second honeymoon and — well . . . you know . . . '

Holly's mother went on and on, waffling from one subject to another until they finally managed to say goodbye. They had talked for forty minutes and Holly hadn't said more than a few words.

However, she did know exactly what her mother meant about Christmas. It needed children to make it really work.

Oh, well. Holly heaved another big sigh that sounded pathetic even to her own ears. She knew how disappointed her mother was at not having grand-children.

But the way things stood, the chances of them ever having a good old traditional Christmas bash with chil-dren entering into the spirit of things were so low as to be non-existent.

Next, Holly phoned her father, but he was so frustrated and preoccupied with his new family it was almost a wasted effort. They hung up amicably enough, but Holly now had a big empty feeling inside her at the prospect of spending Christmas alone.

She did have one or two friends she could have foisted herself off on, but on reflection she thought it might be even lonelier to sit at somebody else's festive table, knowing that she was the odd one out. A single person with no other half to snuggle up to or celebrate with was hardly a prospect that conjured up festive warmth.

4

The strong words Holly planned to have with Joel Richards failed her in the end, and those she did manage to utter fell on decidedly stony ground. Joel was not very receptive to her criticisms about Fred being passed over in favour of someone totally wrong for the part.

'I'm sorry you feel that way, Holly, but the decision is final and that's the end of the matter. Charles Smith is to be the store's new Santa Claus. I won't hear any argument against it.'

'I just don't believe that you could, in all conscience, give the job to a total stranger.'

'Well, that's the way it is.'

He looked agitated and kept glancing at his watch as he spoke.

'Look, Holly, please — just leave it, would you? It may not be for the long term. At this stage I — we don't know . . . '

At that moment, as he was giving Holly the equivalent of the French gallic shrug, his telephone lit up and he grabbed at it as if it was some kind of life-saving device.

As Holly drew in a less than satisfied breath Joel smiled apologetically and immediately went into a discussion on end-of-year profits and new product promotions for the New Year. With a little grunt of exasperation, she stormed out of the office, leaving him to it.

She was in Kay Gregory's office a few minutes later. Kay was the store detective and they were reasonably good friends. She could see immediately that Holly was all keyed up about something.

'What's happened, Holly?' she asked, turning from the rather grubby urchin who was sitting on her typists' chair, revolving slowly and singing to himself in a low, gruff voice. 'You look like you're about to explode.'

'I think I just did, Kay, only nobody took any notice — especially our darling of The Playpen, Mr Richards!'

'Oops!' Kay looked scandalised. 'You haven't fallen out with our new boss, have you?'

Holly lifted her arms and was suddenly aware that there were tight fists at the end of them.

'Oh, Kay! What is it about that man?'

'Everything!' Kay said dreamily, then gave a small, embarrassed laugh when she remembered her small charge. 'Well, we all think he's wonderful.'

'Not all of us, Kay,' Holly butted in indignantly, having no wish to be part of the general consensus of opinion when it came to the new branch manager.

'You don't like him?'

Kay sounded incredulous and Holly just blinked back at her because she couldn't even shake her head. It would be lying — sort of.

'It's personal,' Holly ended up saying, then wished she hadn't because

Kay jumped on her words like a spin-doctor.

'Holly! Are you saying that you and — and Joel Richards . . . ?'

'No, of course not! What a ridiculous idea. He stole my job and now he's done the same to poor old Fred Barnstable.'

'Ah!'

'Don't say 'ah' like that. It makes you sound like a psychologist.'

Kay grinned.

'Well, you have to be a bit of a psychologist in this job. Take our friend here.'

She jerked her thumb over her shoulder and the boy with the dirty face glowered daggers at her back. 'It's the sixth time in the last two weeks he's turned up lost and crying for his mother.'

Holly looked down at the pinched, underfed face of the child who was now puckering up at the mention of his mother.

'But that's awful! Poor little mite.'

'Poor little mite, my foot!' Kay hissed. 'It's his mother who puts him up to it. And while he's distracting my attention she does her shopping.'

'But she could put him in the crèche,' Holly said, then realisation struck home. 'Oh, I see what you mean. She doesn't actually pay for the things she takes.'

'Oh, she'll pay all right, just as soon as I catch her red-handed. When the police finish with her she won't want to do her shopping at The Playpen any more.'

The little boy stopped revolving on the seat and started to cry.

Kay shook her head and pointed to her own eyes. Holly looked back at the child and found that although the weeping sounded and looked genuine enough, there were no tears.

'I see what you mean,' she said with a wry smile, but there was something knotting in her stomach as she looked at the boy.

She doubted that he would be going

home to a good meal and an evening playing computer games — or any other games, for that matter.

'Look, Holly, keep an eye on him for a few minutes, would you?' Kay strolled to the door. 'I need to go to the loo.'

She didn't leave Holly much choice in the matter. Kay was gone before Holly could open her mouth to object.

She and the boy stared blankly at one another. He sniffed and wiped the back of his hand across his face.

'What's your name?' she asked gently, hoping to distract him enough so that he wouldn't think of bolting and therefore get her into trouble with Kay.

'Harry,' he said gruffly and sniffed again.

'Harry what?'

'Just Harry.'

'You must have a second name. My name's Holly Duncan.'

The child simply blinked back at her as if she were speaking a foreign language. She guessed that his mother had warned him never to reveal his full identity if he didn't want to be caught. That was logical, since it would undoubtedly lead to her and possibly an arrest.

'Do you like The Playpen, Harry?' Holly asked, trying to keep it sounding casual.

'It's all right.'

He scratched a knee that shone through a hole in his trousers.

'Well, you must like it, because my friend, Kay, tells me you come in here often with your mother. Does your father ever come with you?'

'I haven't got a father.'

'Oh, that's sad. Everybody needs a father. Are your parents divorced?'

'Uh-uh.' He shook his head and his small blue eyes stared straight ahead unseeingly. 'Mam just has me — and my brothers and sisters.'

'Really? How many brothers and sisters do you have, Harry?'

'Five. Can I go now?'

He was half off the seat, his eyes on the open door.

'I think we'd better wait for Kay, don't you, otherwise we'll both be in trouble. Why does your mother steal things, Harry? She does steal things, doesn't she?'

Harry chewed on his mouth and blinked. This time, the tears that welled up in his eyes were real. Holly saw him swallow hard.

"'Cos she's not got no money and it's Christmas and she wanted to get us kids something nice.'

Then his narrow chest heaved and he was fighting back the sobs that were getting to Holly and making her own eyes sting.

'She wouldn't do it no other time, just at Christmas. She says — she says all the other lads in the world get presents so why shouldn't her kids be happy on Christmas morning.'

Holly leaned forward and offered him a hankie. After a long deliberation, he took it and stuffed it in his pocket, then wiped his face on his sleeve.

'Well, Harry,' she said, perching on

the end of Kay's cluttered desk. 'I think your mother's heart is in the right place, but you do know that it's not right to steal, don't you?'

''Course I do. Mam tells us that all the time.'

'Then tell me. Why does she do it?'

Another loud sniff and his mouth twisted as he replied without looking at Holly in a voice so low that she could barely hear him.

'He pinched all our money and ran off with it, didn't he?'

'Who's that?'

'Eddie, the lodger. Mam said she trusted him, but he did the dirty on her just like all the others.'

'It sounds like your mum is pretty unlucky with her men.'

'Yeah, she is.'

'Do you love her, Harry? Do you love your mum?'

'I suppose so, yeah.'

'And I'm sure she loves you.'

He shrugged and buried his hands deep in his pockets.

'Dunno.'

'She gives you hugs and all that — you're not too big for hugs are you?'

'Dunno.'

'Well, I'd like to bet you're not. I'm a lot bigger than you and I'd give anything for a hug right now.'

'Is that the same as a cuddle?'

'The very same.'

He looked as though he was mulling it over in his mind, his heel all the time tapping on the base of the chair, then he nodded, agreeing to some unspoken thing.

'So why don't you give the lady a cuddle, young man?'

They both jumped at the sound of the voice. Standing in the doorway was Charles Smith, a transformed Charles Smith, complete with red suit and snowy-white beard and rouge-red cheeks.

'Can I?'

Harry's eyes suddenly brightened and shone up at Holly. Before she could do anything about it he threw himself at her and hugged her tightly.

'Well, that was a nice surprise!' she said thickly through an unexpected lump in her throat. He pushed away after a mere two seconds' worth of hugs and grinned sheepishly.

'That's the ticket, young man,' Santa Claus told him.

'My name's Harry!'

'Well, Harry.' The man Holly had disliked so intensely was taking on a far different persona and, she had to admit, looked more genuine in his disguise than Fred ever had. 'Let's see if we can do something for you and your family this Christmas, eh? Come with me, laddie. I have a special grotto for people just like you.'

Harry looked at Holly for confirmation and when she nodded he trotted off happily, holding tightly on to the white-gloved hand.

Holly followed at a distance, signalling to Kay, who had come out of the staff-room and was just about to pounce on a woman hovering at the novelty counter.

The moment Kay's attention was distracted, the woman made a hasty exit, but not before Holly saw the family resemblance and guessed she was young Harry's mother.

'Oh no, Holly! I almost had her then,' Kay complained as Holly grabbed her arm and dragged her to Santa's Grotto. 'What are you up to?'

'Not me — Santa. Come on, let's see how he deals with Harry.'

* * *

Charles Smith dealt extremely well with Harry, as it happened.

The boy's face glowed with excitement as he stood by Santa's knee and Santa scribbled away in his notebook as Harry dictated.

'What's he writing?' Kay wanted to know. 'Fred never used to do that.'

'I suppose he's making notes — taking down Harry's wishes for Christmas, poor kid.'

47

'It'll be a bit of a letdown when Christmas morning dawns and Harry finds nothing more than an apple and an orange in his stocking.'

Harry finished his long talk with Santa Claus and fairly skipped out of the grotto, waving to Charles Smith all the way. Kay took a step forward and Holly could see that she was going to grab the little boy.

She held her back as Harry whizzed past them with eyes shining and a cheeky grin.

'Let him go, Kay. It's Christmas. You know — season of goodwill and all that.' Holly heard her mother's voice coming out of her own mouth and quivered with internal laughter.

Kay sighed.

'You know, Holly Duncan, you try to fool us all that you're pretty hard boiled, but I figure you're just an old softy at heart.'

Holly tossed her a careless smile.

'Well, keep it to yourself. I'd hate my reputation to be ruined.'

5

The atmosphere between Holly and Joel remained professional and cool. A little too cool, Holly thought, but what could she expect? She had given him nothing but an icy reception right from the start.

By the end of that week, Joel did actually ask her what she thought of the new Santa Claus.

'Does he come up to your very high standards, Holly?'

His smile was slightly sarcastic and she felt her hackles rise sharply.

'He seems to be doing an adequate job and . . . ' She had to give in to the more positive side of Charles Smith. 'Well, to be quite honest, I never thought he would look the part, but he does. He's even better with the children than Fred was.'

'And, of course, the beard is real.'

'Yes. It's been put to the test on more than one occasion. You'd be surprised how much strength a three-year-old has who is determined to prove something.'

Joel's head went back and he laughed heartily. Holly was surprised to find herself laughing alongside him and when they got over their mirth they stared at one another and there followed a long, awkward silence.

'Holly . . . ?'

'Yes, Joel?'

'Miss Loach told me that you questioned my motives over the hiring of Charles Smith.'

'Yes, I did.'

Holly locked eyes with him, but he didn't flinch.

'The poor woman is feeling guilty for letting it drop that there is some deeply-guarded secret that she is not at liberty to divulge.'

'Perhaps she is not the one who should be feeling guilty.'

'You're quite right and I'd be obliged if you wouldn't badger her — or anybody else — on the subject. Just do your job, Holly, and let me do mine.'

Holly could feel her hackles rising afresh.

'And what if this so-called secret of yours impinges on my job, Joel? What then?'

He looked thoughtful and tapped a tattoo on his desk with his long fingers. Holly heard him sigh deeply.

'Don't worry, Holly,' he said eventually. 'We're not exactly dealing with underworld crime you know. Nobody's going to take a pot shot at you just because you get too nosy.'

'Oh, very funny.' Holly gave a brittle laugh and wished he hadn't said that. 'I'd just like to know what I'm involved in, that's all. I think you owe me that, at least.'

'You're not involved in anything, Holly. What's happening is entirely my business, not yours.'

'And Charles Smith?'

He pointed a finger at her and she almost felt the jet of lightning it sent

51

out like a laser beam.

'If you say anything to Charles Smith — anything at all, Holly, that you wouldn't have said to Fred Barnstable — I will have you out of your job and out of this store so fast your feet won't touch the ground. Do I make myself clear?'

'Perfectly!'

★   ★   ★

Maybe she should have done what he told her and kept well out of it, but Holly's curiosity was too strong to allow her to turn a blind eye and sit on her laurels.

Besides, what else did she have to do?

Her life at that particular time had ground down to a big fat boring zero, so turning herself into some kind of latter-day Miss Marple gave her some interest and put a spark of excitement in her heart.

After her conversation with Joel, Holly kept a more than watchful eye on

Charles Smith, but he never put a foot out of line.

He was, it had to be said, most successful as Santa Claus.

He was popular with children of all ages and the parents liked him, too. There was something so very genuine about him and it was a lot more than the beard.

About a week before Christmas, there were reports in the local papers about a spate of burglaries. Holly didn't think much of it at first. This kind of thing always presented itself at Christmas.

Thieves knew that houses were rich with new presents waiting to be given. They hung about, waiting for people to go out on their seasonal social whirls and then they struck.

The burglaries were brought closer to home when one or two of the shop's customers reported that they had been victims of this heartless crime. Holly overheard a group of regulars talking about it with great animation.

When they saw her they waved her over. Three out of five had been hit by burglaries, two of them on days when they had been shopping at The Playpen.

'It's getting worse,' one elderly granny wagged her head scandalously. 'Nobody's safe these days. They even do it in broad daylight.'

'If you ask me,' a young pregnant mother said, 'they've got inside information.'

Something icy crept down Holly's spine. She looked towards Santa's Grotto where she could see three young children gathered around Charles Smith, who was busily writing things down as they watched with wide-eyed anticipation.

She waited until the children came out of the grotto, then approached them as they were picked up by their parents.

'Did you enjoy talking to Santa Claus?' she asked with a bright, encouraging smile.

Three heads nodded vigorously.

'What did he ask you?'

The eldest sucked in her cheeks, took a deep breath and told her.

'He wanted to know what we wanted for Christmas. Then we had to give him our address so he could programme it into his computer and his reindeers would know where to deliver things on Christmas Eve.'

'I see! Well, that's very efficient of him, isn't it? I hope you get what you want.'

'We love coming into your shop,' the mother said, picking up her youngest and giving her a cuddle. 'I just wish things weren't so expensive. Still, we've warned the children not to expect too much this year.'

Holly hoped that the children would understand, but was doubtful. It was hard being a parent these days if you didn't have money, and a lot of the local men were out of work.

6

By the end of that day Holly made up her mind to follow Charles Smith when he left the shop. It was dark and freezing and the first fluffy blanket of snow was floating down, making everything look even more seasonal.

She hadn't realised how difficult it was to follow a car that merged into the traffic and became one with the black, greasy road surface and spectacle of dazzling red taillights. Twice, she thought she had lost him, then she had to drop back slightly on finding herself right behind him.

Once out of the hustle of Newcastle it became easier and Holly was able to leave a bigger gap between them. Mr Smith headed towards the Ponteland Road.

His house, she found, was a large red brick Victorian manor house, which did not altogether surprise her.

What did surprise her was how gloomy and empty it seemed. There were no welcoming lights, no welcoming voices as he put his key in the latch and let himself in.

Almost immediately, a light came on in what was undoubtedly the sitting-room. Holly crept up the drive, thankful that he didn't have a dog, and stood on tiptoe to peer inside.

When the telephone shrilled out, Holly jumped and flattened herself against the wall with a little gasp.

'Yes,' she heard Charles Smith's muffled voice through the diamond-paned windows. 'I have some more addresses for you. You've done the necessary with the last list, I hope. Good. I'll see you later then.'

Determined to see whom he was planning to meet later on and pass those addresses on to, Holly huddled down in her car, which was discreetly parked across the road.

Within minutes her teeth were

chattering with the cold. Next time she came out sleuthing, she told herself, she would come prepared with a flask of coffee and some thermal underwear.

Fortunately, she didn't have long to wait. A car drew up and a tall, familiar figure got out, glancing briefly about him.

The snow was falling more thickly now, but Holly had no difficulty in recognising the man who let himself into Charles Smith's house with his own key.

It was Joel Richards.

★　★　★

Holly stayed in the car outside Charles Smith's house for as long as she could tolerate the cold.

She was frozen stiff and tired by the time she turned on the ignition and drove away almost silently on the thick carpet of new snow.

Joel hadn't reappeared and it was almost ten o'clock. Whatever business he had with the mysterious Santa Claus, it was taking some time to sort out. Rather than wait till she got home to her cold flat to eat, she stopped on the way and treated herself to fish and chips and a cup of tea.

It did a lot to revive her, but not enough to build up a morale that was definitely on a downward curve.

Once home, Holly turned up the heating to full power and went around still in her sheepskin jacket and boots until she warmed through thoroughly, by which time it was getting on for midnight.

Her mind was far too busy to think of sleep, so she dragged out her various boxes of Christmas decorations and spent the next couple of hours making the place look festive and jolly, thinking it might lift her mood out of the morass into which it had fallen. She had previously decided not to bother this year. It seemed so futile, being the only one to see it.

It was almost a year to the day that

Holly's last relationship had broken up. It had hurt to make the decision to split with Doug, but she could see that the relationship didn't have enough to offer her. It would have been so easy just to go along with the tide.

Fortunately, she realised before it was too late that their individual tides were flowing in opposite directions.

Besides, she was always too busy playing the career girl, taking on more and more responsibility, working all hours just to prove that she was worthy of the job. Boyfriends, no matter how nice they were, tended to get in the way of her ambitions.

All the talk about women being equal was all right, but the men she went out with still preferred their women to earn less than they did and occupy less important positions.

Not that her position was hugely important, but everybody told her she was going places and until recently she had never doubted this fact.

Not until Joel Richards came on the

scene. In one fell swoop the new handsome hero of the toyshop world had put a block on her promotion and stepped right into the job himself. And now he was hob-nobbing with a mysterious stranger who was almost certainly a criminal.

Holly heaved a deep-felt sigh and looked around her. Flats were such lonely places in which to live, she thought. Had she been appointed as branch manager she would have been able to afford to buy a small house with a garden.

That had also been part of the dream. She longed to have a dog, too; a nice, friendly, furry companion that wouldn't betray her or blame her for anything. She could go for long walks with him and . . .

Goodness, what was the use of thinking about what might have been? She was getting maudlin and she didn't like it. Another sigh and she found herself staring morosely out of the window down into the street below where the roads were shining an oily black beneath a bleak, wintry sky.

Cars hissed by taking their owners home. She wondered bleakly how many of them out there went home to empty flats and houses and talked to themselves or turned the television up high to counteract the loneliness.

'Holly,' she told her mirrored image in the window, 'this kind of thinking is not good for you. It's too negative. You have to do something with your life. What's the use of getting depressed? That solves nothing at all.'

Maybe, she thought, I should settle for a cat or, like Miss Loach, a budgie or a canary!

Holly reached for the phone and punched in Doug's number. She didn't know why she did it. There were other numbers she could have rung, but that was the only one that registered in her brain.

It rang out a few times and she listened, her heart jumping slightly, because she didn't know what she would say to him if he answered. Maybe he would think her all kinds of a fool. He was probably busy anyway.

'Hello?'

The familiar voice in her ear made her jump and it really did seem that her heart had stopped beating altogether. He repeated the greeting, sounding only vaguely curious, then hung up. Holly hadn't said a word.

Everyone said you should never go back, that things would never be as good as the first time. Maybe they were right. She was sure they were right. He hadn't been the right man for her then and he wasn't the kind of man to change. He was far too cemented in his ways. Perhaps she was, too.

No doubt, she told herself, feeling the hint of a warm flush, Joel Richards would be just as rigid. Not that she would ever be close enough to him to want to change him. Heaven forbid!

7

On the following Monday, Joel came into the store late. Holly was already up to her ears in lost children, distraught mothers and a few irate fathers, so she wasn't too pleased to be summoned to their shared office in a rather abrupt manner.

'Can we talk please, Holly? In the office, now!'

She made her apologies to the Bird family who were desperately trying to replace some items that had been stolen during a burglary at the weekend so their children would have something to wake up to on Christmas morning.

'I do hope you get things sorted out,' Holly said to them.

'Well,' Mrs Bird said, frowning deeply, 'at least the burglar suffered for his pains.'

'Oh?' She hesitated, aware of Joel

standing at the other side of the shop in the open doorway of their office. 'How's that?'

'Well, you see, he must have fallen in his hurry when he heard the dog barking and crashed through the glass-topped coffee table — another worry for the insurance man! There was blood everywhere, so he must have cut himself.'

'How awful for you.'

By the time Holly joined Joel, his impatience was showing.

'I really don't have time to wait while you indulge in social chit-chat,' he snapped as she closed the office door behind her.

She managed to give him a withering look.

'It wasn't social chit-chat, as you call it. I was simply doing my job and trying to help the Bird family, who are regular customers here. They were burgled at the weekend and lost all their Christmas presents.'

'Really? There seems to be a lot of it

about at the moment.'

He looked momentarily abashed by his off-handed manner.

'I'm sorry, Holly, but we have an urgent situation on our hands. Miss Loach is absent. Flu, apparently, and, since she always takes the key to her filing cabinet home with her and no-one seems to know the password to access her computer records, I wondered if you knew where we could contact Fred Barnstable.'

'Fred? Why? I thought you didn't want him working here.'

'The fact is that Charles Smith is also unwell and we really can't afford to be without a Santa Claus. I called the agency, but they don't have anybody spare.'

'I know where to find him,' Holly said and saw relief flood his face. 'He's got a flat in Jesmond. The landlord — well, he's an old friend of mine.'

Holly didn't want to explain that Doug Hillman was also her ex-partner. They had met three years ago when she was trying to find somewhere for Fred to live after the poor man suddenly found himself on the street.

Doug was a nice man and for a long time she thought she was in love with him, but it hadn't worked out. It was just one of those things.

'I'd be grateful, Holly,' Joel said, putting his hand on her shoulder, 'if you would ask Fred to stand in for Charles Smith. That is, if he's not too busy . . . '

'Or too proud?' Holly glanced sideways to avoid his penetrating stare and that's when she noticed the bandage on his hand. She blinked at it, then stared up at him. 'What happened to your hand?'

He withdrew it quickly.

'Oh, that! It's not as bad as it looks. I had an argument with a cat. She needed rescuing, but didn't appreciate that I was the rescue service. The scratch turned septic, hence the bandage.'

'Oh, I see.'

Holly went to her own desk and sat down, reaching for the phone.

'Well, I'd better phone Doug and ask him to do some sweet-talking to Fred.'

★ ★ ★

'Penny for 'em. Holly, love!'

Holly was nibbling on the end of her pen and deep in thought about rich con men, burglaries and bandaged hands, so she didn't hear Fred come into the office.

'Fred! Oh, am I glad to see you!'

'I know somebody who would be ecstatic to see you, gal.'

Fred wiped a large handkerchief over his blue-veined nose and his eyes twinkled mischievously.

'So how is Doug, then?' Holly asked, not sure if she really wanted to know, because the last time she enquired after him he had just announced his engagement to someone else.

'Pining, I'd say,' Fred told her. 'He sends his love and wants to know what you're doing for Christmas. Seems he's broken up with that fiancée of his. You still hankering after him, eh?'

She shook her head.

'No, Fred, of course not.'

What a relief to be able to say that and really mean it, she thought. Although she was a bit lonely and miserable, there were definitely no candles still burning for Doug and she was sorry if it wasn't the same for him.

'So, it seems they need their old Santa Claus after all,' Fred said with a derisive sniff.

'That's about it, Fred.'

Holly nodded and frowned because she could still see Joel's bandaged hand and hear Mrs Bird talking about the burglar who had cut himself.

'Well, I'll get stuck in then.' Fred was heading for the shop floor. 'My old costume in the same place, is it?'

★   ★   ★

A few minutes later, Fred, now in his red disguise, wandered back in and handed Charles Smith's outfit to Holly, which he had found crushed in his locker.

'Won't do it no good in there, Holly. This material creases something rotten. Thought I'd better give it to you to keep for him. It might need an iron before it'll be fit to wear again.'

She took it from him and he went off, loping across the store, whistling happily under his false beard, obviously more than a little glad to be back.

Holly draped the red costume over the back of a spare chair and as she did so, the famous notebook fell from one of the voluminous pockets.

At first she simply laid it on the corner of the desk, then a warm feeling crept through her, causing a slight rise of butterflies. She fingered the book for a moment or two, then flipped it open.

The pages were full of names, addresses and items listed under **Presents Wanted**. Dozens and dozens of them, the Bird family included.

Lots of the earlier recorded addresses had a large tick scored through them. Had she perhaps stumbled on the answer to the mystery — and to the epidemic of burglaries? It was a daunting thought.

Holly shot a quick glance at Joel's calendar and saw that he was due to be at a shareholders' meeting, so there was little likelihood of him walking in on her when she was doing yet another bit of detective work.

She found most of the ticked addresses in the telephone directory and, with the excuse that they were letting their customers know personally that they would be staying open late during the last days running up to Christmas, she also managed to ask if they had been free of burglaries so far, just a casual question tossed in after the sales talk.

Not one of the houses contacted had been burgled. Holy couldn't believe it. She had been so sure that this was

Charles Smith's little game. So sure, in fact, that she had been ready to sacrifice her job for it.

Thinking that she had perhaps misread the clues, she phoned the people who had no tick against their names.

Only one family in that group had been burgled and that, they said, was at least two months ago, long before Charles Smith had occupied Santa's Grotto.

Holly was just coming to the end of the list when Joel strolled in. He looked and sounded tired. It had been a long, hard meeting and he had missed lunch because of it.

When he told her that, she glanced at her watch and gasped at how quickly the time had passed while she was occupied on the phone.

'I haven't eaten either,' she said.

'In that case, come on.'

He was taking down her coat from the peg on the far wall and holding it out to her.

'Let's go and grab a sandwich and something to drink at the pub over the road. I'm whacked and you look like you've had a frenetic day so far.'

Holly saw him grinning slightly at her and knew exactly what state she must be in. While on the phone she had the tendency to run her fingers through her hair. It was almost certainly standing on end after the long telephone session she had just had.

'It's been busy,' she confirmed, trying to flatten down the rampant tendrils to something resembling her normal coiffure, which was natural fuzz rather than chic.

'Leave it,' he ordered, pulling her hand down. 'It suits you like that and, well, I quite like the windswept look.'

Holly thought it probably looked like windswept candyfloss, but she didn't like to make a fuss, especially after what he had said.

As she grabbed her bag and started to follow him out of the office, she noticed the notebook and picked it up.

'By the way, this fell out of Charles Smith's Santa Claus pocket.'

He seemed to do a double take, then quickly recovered himself.

'Oh? Well, he'll be back in a couple of days no doubt. Let me lock it in my desk for safe keeping.'

Holly frowned at his outstretched hand and hesitated a long time before placing the book in his broad palm. She could have kept it just as safe in her own desk, but she wasn't in the mood to argue.

★   ★   ★

There was a blizzard blowing outside and just getting from one side of the street to the other was quite a business. Joel gripped Holly's arm just above the elbow and practically carried her across.

They sat in a corner of the pub where there was an infra-red wall heater and he ordered two ploughman's and a couple of double whisky-Macs.

'I normally only drink wine,' she told him, slightly annoyed that he hadn't even asked what she wanted.

'So do I, but I felt the need for something a bit stronger.' Then he gave his wide, boyish grin. 'Don't look so worried, Holly. I have no intention of getting you drunk. Well, not at three o'clock in the afternoon, anyway.'

'And at no other time, I would hope,' she couldn't help adding.

However, Holly found that the whisky drink was incredibly warming and by the time she was halfway down the glass and two-thirds through the huge, crusty bread sandwich, she was feeling almost light-hearted, which was a bit disconcerting given the strangeness of the situation.

'Tell me, Joel,' Holly started to speak, then had to repeat it because her voice had belted out loudly and one or two people turned to see what she was shouting at. 'Why is Charles Smith taking note of all our customers' addresses? I mean, that's not required. It's not as if he really needs to know where any of the children lives.'

'Being as how Santa Claus knows everything without being told?' His face dimpled and he indicated to the barman that they would like two coffees. 'It's just his way of doing things, Holly. Don't worry your head about it.'

'But I am worried.' There was that now familiar teeth-gritting irritation, though it was somewhat watered down today — by the whisky no doubt. 'I mean — well, there've been all those burglaries and — and . . . '

'And what?'

Holly was staring at his injured hand and daring herself to accuse him, or at least let him know that she was suspicious.

'Oh, nothing!' She sighed, her courage failing her. 'It's just my imagination running away with itself.'

He studied her carefully over the rim of his coffee cup.

'Your cheeks are prettily pink, Holly,' he said suddenly and she felt her eyes stretch as wide as they could go as he leaned over the tiny table towards her. 'And your lips are seductively red, like sweet ripe cherries.'

Their faces were so close they were almost touching. Holly's heart did a kind of uncomfortable flip and she let the tip of her tongue dart out and lick the very lips he was talking about.

She knew she should have backed off, but she just didn't think about it. There she was, in broad daylight, in front of the whole world, and she was being kissed by Joel Richards, the man she most liked to hate, a charmer and almost certainly a conman.

And, horror of horrors, she was actually enjoying the feel of his mouth pressed on hers and the way his hand closed over her fingers and squeezed them just tight enough to make her want more.

Somebody cleared his throat and

they sprung apart to find the barman standing there looking highly amused.

'You two lovebirds want more coffee then?' he asked with a grin.

Joel looked at Holly and laughed.

'No, thanks,' he said, casting his eyes to the ceiling. 'But keep that mistletoe handy. We might be back.'

Holly followed his gaze and saw the gently swinging bunch of mistletoe with its pale helicopter leaves and its creamy white berries.

'Well, really!' she gasped and heard Joel laughing again.

'Sorry, Holly. I just couldn't resist it. Now, I think it's time we got back to work, don't you?'

'Yes, I do!'

'And, Holly — just forget that notebook, eh? It doesn't mean anything to anyone but Charles Smith.'

'If you say so.'

Her reply was a little clipped. Had the kiss really been to soften her up, to sweeten her? Perhaps he thought that he could charm her into looking away while he and Smith cheated innocent people out of their Christmas.

Suddenly she was no longer sure of anything.

8

Charles Smith came back to work two days later, though they all agreed that he did not look at all well. He had the grey, worried look of a man with something serious on his mind, though he could still raise a smile and a twinkle in the eye as soon as he was dealing with the children.

Holly watched him closely, hating herself for suspecting him of anything untoward. He was so good with those kids and his enjoyment in the rôle of Santa Claus was genuine, she was sure of that. Just now and then she caught a hint of underlying problems. Whether it was something physical or a guilty conscience that was stabbing him, she had no idea.

'Don't fuss, my dear,' he said when Holly suggested he had come back too soon and should take another day or two to recover from whatever ailed him. 'I feel better than I've felt in a long time and it has a lot to do with working here at The Playpen. People are so friendly — so kind.'

Holly had to admit to herself that she, too, was glad to see him once more don the red suit with the fluffy white trim, even though it meant that poor Fred was being pushed out in the cold, yet again.

There had been an endless stream of children and their parents badgering her and wanting to know when the nice, tubby little Santa was coming back.

She prayed that her suspicions were simply the result of an overactive imagination, and her harsh judgement had been brought on by resentment at having to step aside and make way for the handsome and much-admired Joel Richards.

'Did Joel return your notebook, Mr Smith?' she asked and he gave her a thoughtful little smile, patting his capacious pocket to reassure himself.

'Yes.' He nodded. 'I was worried in case I had lost it. When I left here that night, I was feeling so unwell that I simply forgot it.'

'Well, it wouldn't have been too drastic,' she suggested, but he looked quite horrified at that.

'Oh, but yes!' He patted his pocket again where the book was obviously residing. 'This little book is more important to me than you could ever know.'

Holly didn't say anything to that, just blinked at him and he hurried off on hearing a buzz of children's voices calling from his grotto.

★　★　★

In the days that followed, the shop saw double the normal number of children queuing to see their favourite Santa Claus, so he had to be doing something right. Holly just wished that her suspicions about him were not going to be proved correct.

Even that young ragamuffin, Harry, popped in, this time without his mother. He got his eye on Holly and smiled bashfully as he stuffed his hands deep inside his pockets and shuffled his feet.

'Hi there, Harry!' She went over to him and ruffled his short-cropped hair. 'You're not doing the family shopping, I hope?'

'Nah! Anyway, I never took anything.' Then he flushed crimson and pulled her handkerchief out of his ragged pocket and held it out to her. 'Well, except this. I thought it was a nice present for me mam, but . . . sorry, miss. I didn't really mean to steal it.'

Holly smiled broadly.

'I gave it to you anyway, Harry,' she told him and his eyebrows shot up. 'You keep it, for being honest. Let's see if we can find you a pretty piece of paper to wrap it in, eh?'

'Aw, miss!'

He looked completely taken aback.

After a stunned moment, he darted forward and gave her a quick hug. When he looked up she saw that his eyes were brimming with real tears.

That makes two hugs I've had this year, Holly thought wistfully, as Harry walked proudly out of the shop clutching his precious parcel and an additional bag of sweets for his brothers and sisters.

She sighed and thought she must indeed be getting soft in her old age or something.

Having children had never been part of her plan of things, but something inside her was changing.

Maybe, she thought, she was getting broody. She certainly got a catch in her throat these days when she saw men with babies or even young couples kissing.

'There you are, Holly!' Joel startled her out of her deep thoughts. 'Look, there's another crisis at home and I have to go. I know I can leave you in charge. After all, you know the job better than I do.'

'Oh, does that mean you won't be here for the staff party on Christmas Eve?' she said.

Joel shook his head and Holly wondered why she should feel disappointed rather than elated. After all, she was far more relaxed when he wasn't around. His presence, especially at a social event, would undoubtedly cause far too much emotional turmoil.

'It doesn't look like it,' Joel said. 'I'm sure you'll all have a great time, but make sure they don't get too drunk and wreck the place — or play with the toys.'

'I'll do my best. Is someone ill, then?' Holly wasn't usually nosy, but she really did think he should be able to trust her sufficiently to keep her informed, even on a personal level.

He drew in a long breath and hesitated, then, 'I — um — I have a daughter in London. She lives with my parents — her mother, too — I mean, we all . . . '

The telephone started to ring and he scowled at it.

'It's a big family home and we sort of all live together in it . . . '

The news landed like a brick in the pit of Holly's stomach.

He was married and a father and he had kissed her knowing that. That made her feel really cheap. Not only that, he was probably mixed up in something illegal and whatever it was she would be a fool to get involved. She should tell the police, but what could she offer as evidence?

The telephone was still ringing. He grabbed up the receiver and barked his name into it, then was immediately apologetic to the person at the other end.

'Sorry! Didn't mean to bite your head off. What? A bad day? Yes, I suppose you could say that. Yes, fine — I'm on my way. See you tomorrow.' He replaced the receiver and shot Holly a curious smile. 'Well, have a happy Christmas, Holly.'

'You, too.' She didn't know why she should have felt so hurt at his apparent indifference. As had happened so often over the past few weeks, they stood there, for what seemed an age, looking at one another like a couple of stone statues. 'Well, you'd better go, then.'

His head shot up as if his thoughts had been miles away.

'Yes — right.'

Then he was gone and Holly was struggling with a hot flush of confusion. She sat down behind her desk and tried to apply her mind to some paperwork, but nothing seemed to unblock her head.

Two minutes later the phone rang again. Holly picked it up.

'Hello?' She could have kicked herself for sounding so vague to the caller on the other end. 'I'm sorry — how can I help you?'

'Who is this? Is my husband still there?'

It was a rather shrill, officious female voice.

'Your husband?'

'Joel Richards, of course! I've just been speaking to him — oh, for goodness' sake, girl, put me on to someone with authority, will you? This is urgent.'

Holly gulped and felt her fingers stiffen as they gripped the phone so hard it hurt.

'I am the authority around here in Joel's absence, Mrs Richards,' she managed to say as levelly as she could, ashamed that she had given the impression of incompetence, especially to Joel's wife. 'He's already left the store. Perhaps you can try to get him at home later.'

'No, never mind. Is Uncle Charles still there?'

'I beg your pardon?'

'Uncle Charles — Charles Richards. I thought he worked there or something.'

'I'm sorry, there's no-one here by that name — oh!'

Pieces of the puzzle were slowly

beginning to fit together, though there was still a lot to be solved.

'Are you talking about a stocky man with bright blue eyes and a beard?'

'That's him, yes. What kind of position do you hold in the store if you can't remember the owner's name, Miss . . . ?'

Holly gagged. Owner! Just what little game was Charles Richards, alias Charles Smith, alias Santa Claus playing? And what part was his nephew, Joel, playing in the same game?

She had never hung up on anyone before, but she hung up on Joel's wife right then and sat staring at the phone for a long time.

If looks could kill the poor instrument would have been dead within seconds, she thought morosely.

How many more lies and mysteries were there, she wondered. It was just too bad of him to . . . to what? She didn't really know what Joel had done, nor his famous uncle.

Oh, yes, she had heard of Charles

Richards and his millions. He was a confirmed bachelor and lived the life, according to the gossip columns, of a bitter old hermit.

Well, well! Just think of it. Charles Richards, a latter day Scrooge, playing the part of Santa Claus. It was absurd and totally bizarre.

Holly let her fingers trail over the telephone. In her mind she was back in the pub with Joel. She was experiencing again that kiss and, even though he made light of it, blaming the presence of the mistletoe, Holly could have sworn she was not the only one to feel something electric pass between them.

Why had he not told her that he had a wife back in London? A wife and a child, for goodness' sake! Just what kind of man was Joel Richards and what were he and his uncle really up to?

★   ★   ★

'You can't really suspect him of . . . of . . . '

'That's just it.' Holly looked at Kay as they sat drinking coffee together and eating chocolates in Thornton's Coffee House. 'I don't know what they're up to, the pair of them, but it's something dishonest, I'm sure.'

'Go on with you!' Kay wasn't in the mood to be swayed away from her admiration of Joel Richards or Charles Smith. 'Those two are the best thing that's happened to The Playpen for as long as I can remember.'

'I know! I know, Kay! At least, that's what everybody keeps telling me. Especially you.'

'Look, Holly, if you go around making wild accusations against Joel it'll only look like sour grapes because he got your job and you feel miffed about the whole thing.'

Kay reached out, her fingers hovering anxiously over the last chocolate on the plate between them. 'Do you like strawberry parfait?'

'No, you go ahead. I've had more than enough apricot pralines and far too many coffee creams.'

'Like I said . . . ' Kay quickly popped the chocolate in her mouth and deliciously licked her fingers. 'The worst thing you could do is start some sort of hate campaign. It won't do you any good at all.'

'But what if they are doing something illegal? Kay, I'd never live with myself if I let them get away with it. It would be tantamount to being an accomplice.'

Kay laughed and wiped her mouth free of chocolate.

'I think you watch too many late-night movies. You should get out more. Get a life, Holly.'

Get a life, indeed! Wasn't that exactly what she had been doing? Now, everything in her day-to-day existence revolved around life before and after Joel Richards.

'You don't believe me, do you?' Holly suggested to her friend.

Kay heaved a huge sigh and looked wistfully over at the chocolate counter.

'You tell me that our new Santa has

been collecting addresses from the kids and seems to have some kind of relationship with our new manager, who visited him at his home. And you think you heard them saying things that don't make sense. Oh, Holly, of course I believe you, but quite honestly, I don't see the point in all this digging around you seem to be doing.'

'So what do you think I should do? You are, after all, in charge of security at the store.'

'Yes, but I can't do anything without concrete evidence.'

'So, I just sit back and let them get away with it?'

'Get away with what?'

'I don't know!'

'See what I mean?' Kay patted Holly's shoulder as she got up and headed for the door. 'My advice is just leave well alone and let it all come out in the wash. Don't stick your neck out unless you have absolute proof that a crime is being committed. Otherwise, my girl, you might end up losing more than your job.'

'Oh, really! Now who's imagining things?'

Holly grabbed her shopping and followed Kay out of the shop, wishing she had kept quiet about the whole thing, wishing even more that she had never put two and two together and come up with a hundred.

But most of all, she was wishing she was not falling in love with Joel Richards, if that's what it was. Kay had suggested that she was going through a bad time because she was missing Doug. Maybe she was right. Maybe, after all, she had these feelings for Joel because she was on the rebound.

Well, if that's the way things were, it was going to have to stop. And right now. Rebound affairs only led to more trouble and misery and she had had enough of that. She would just have to make sure that her heart was firmly closed to the handsome and married manager of The Playpen.

9

It was surprisingly easy for Holly to fool herself into believing that she was miserable because she really was missing Doug after all.

She felt bad about walking out on him the way she had. And she had certainly entertained second thoughts, but by the time she got round to telling him about it, he had already taken up with someone else. Now, he was free once more and, by all accounts, willing to try again with her.

Feeling a twinge of conscience, and something else she could not define, she finally rang Doug, and invited him to the staff Christmas party.

It wasn't an event she ever looked forward to with much enthusiasm. Seeing people you worked with, minus their inhibitions and plus their partners, isn't always such a pleasing experience when you were all alone and not too happy.

'Do you mean — like a date?'

There was a note of hesitancy in Doug's voice and she could tell he was trying desperately not to sound too enthusiastic.

'If you like,' she said. 'You don't have to come, you know — only if you have nothing better to do. Of course, if there's . . . '

'I'll come! Of course, I'll come!'

★   ★   ★

Doug arrived early at her flat, which immediately put her in a bad mood. He had never been strong on time-keeping all the while they were together, but he usually erred on the late side.

As it was, Holly was only half ready when he was standing outside her door ringing the bell.

'Doug!'

She was clutching her housecoat around her, having just stepped out of the shower with her hair in taming rubber curlers and her face thick with green clay that was supposed to keep wrinkles at bay.

'Go and drive around the block a few dozen times, will you? I need time to metamorphose.'

'It's freezing out there!'

He shoved a bunch of rather jaded chrysanthemums into Holly's arms and gently pushed past her into the warmth of the flat.

'Anyway, I've seen you looking worse.'

'Oh, thank you!'

She sniffed at the flowers, hiding a grimace behind his back, at the same time noticing that he was still wearing the casual jeans and sweater that she remembered so well. Dressing up for an occasion was not in Doug's nature.

As for his rather tactless remark . . . was it something to do with being an ex that allowed men to no longer speak reverently, admiringly and, at the very least, tactfully, when they were in your presence, she wondered.

She banged the front door shut and shuffled after him in her fluffy bunny slippers. He marched into the living-room and made himself at home.

'You've made a few changes, I see,' he said, letting his eyes wander around the walls and through the open door into the kitchen.

'For the better, I think.'

Doug gave her a look.

'I understood you had someone else in your life, Holly. I don't see any sign of him.'

'You won't, because there isn't anyone,' she shouted from the bath-room where she was frantically trying to divest herself of the green facial gunge without getting it into her hair. 'Anyway, you're the one who got engaged pretty quickly after we split up. What happened to her?'

There was a short silence and Holly could hear him moving about restlessly because the leather of her new settee was creaking loudly.

'She wanted us to go and be missionaries in some distant and very foreign land. I couldn't cut it, so I opted out.'

'You don't sound too sorry about it.'

Holly thought she was going to be streaked with green mud for evermore. She groaned at herself in the bathroom mirror, thinking what a pity it wasn't Hallowe'en instead of Christmas Eve.

'I'm not. I just got engaged to her to make you jealous.'

'Oh? That seems a bit drastic to me.'

Well, it had worked at first, but Holly wasn't going to admit that. What she was admitting to herself right then was that she really had been over Doug for a long time now. Seeing him again like this confirmed it.

She didn't want to go back down that uncertain road. Actually, he was always certain. Holly was the one who could never make up her mind whether she wanted him or not.

So, she told her dismal reflection, there definitely was no question of being on the rebound. He had hardly been back two minutes and she knew, without a shadow of a doubt, that what she thought she felt for Joel Richards — though she was desperately trying to deny it — had nothing to do with Doug.

★ ★ ★

As Holly was having another attempt at swilling off the facial mask she heard the doorbell yet again and grappled about blindly for the towel.

'Shall I get it?' Doug wanted to know.

'Please! I've got this stuff in my eyes now and it hurts like the dickens.'

She heard the click of the door and a mutter of voices, but the taps were still running water and Holly couldn't make anything out.

When she came out of the bathroom, red-faced and red-eyed, blinking away the tears and blowing her nose on loo paper, she thought she was hallucinating.

100

There, looking totally out of place, was Joel Richards, a spray of red roses in one hand, a bottle of champagne in the other.

And Doug was staring at him in something of a seething way. She could almost hear his teeth grinding.

'Joel! What on earth are you doing here? I thought you were going to be in London until after Christmas.'

He gave her a quick smile that disappeared as soon as he looked at Doug. Doug scowled back at him.

'So did I, but the plan changed at the last minute and . . . ' He was frowning at Holly and she remembered the state she was in. 'Have I called at a bad time? I just thought that we could have — um — coupled up for the staff party, but I can see it was a bad idea.'

He shot another glance at Doug and Holly could see what he was thinking.

There she was, partially clad, red-faced and crying — or that's how it must have looked to him.

She gave a half-hearted laugh and

decided that perhaps she was safer with the two of them rather than either one on their own.

'Don't be silly! The more the merrier. I was just . . . ' Holly indicated her face with a waggle of fingers. 'Doug arrived about an hour too soon and caught me a thousand miles off-guard, if you can be miles off guard, but you know what I mean, I'm sure . . . '

Oh, goodness, she was babbling, and the more nervous she became the more she babbled, and the redder her face became.

Doug didn't seem to notice, but she saw Joel's wide mouth twist as if he was trying not to laugh.

'We have plenty of time,' he said and looked about him. 'Where are your glasses? I thought we might as well get in the party spirit before we arrived.'

Holly chuckled as she dived back into the bathroom to try and patch up the damage with a few subtle cosmetics.

Thankfully, her party frock was hanging behind the door, having had its creases steamed out.

'What a good idea,' she shouted through the now closed door.

'So, where are your glasses? This champagne's beginning to warm up.'

'I'll get them,' she heard Doug say and how she wished she had changed the cupboard where she had always kept 'their' glasses.

★   ★   ★

At last, Holly was ready and made her entrance as boldly as she could. After all, it was her place and neither of her escorts for the evening owned one piece of it — or of her.

They both stared at her as if some alien had just walked through the wall and materialised before them. Doug's reaction was easy to read. She had forgotten how much he detested the colour red, whereas she loved it.

Joel was caught in the middle of pouring champagne into one of the tall flute glasses and she watched, fascinated, as the foaming bubbles overflowed the glass and ran over his fingers.

'Oh, dear! Doug, quick!' Holly pointed a finger in the direction of the kitchen. 'There's a roll of paper towel on the bench.'

He didn't take very long to locate the kitchen roll, but it was long enough for Joel to stare a bit harder, then smile ever so slowly with seductively narrowed eyes.

'You look fantastic, Holly,' he said softly, then his eyes flashed at Doug who was clumsily trying to mop up the spilled champagne from the rug. 'Doesn't she, Doug?'

'What?' Doug's head bobbed up, but he really didn't focus on anything. 'Yes — great! But then, she always does.'

Nice one, Doug, Holly congratulated her ex-boyfriend silently.

The champagne was delicious, though she knew that Doug would have preferred lager. She found a few nibbles to help soak up the alcohol, but by the time the bottle was empty, they were floating gently.

And, she thought, Joel had expected the two of them to drink all that!

'Right, shall we go, then?' Joel seemed in better spirits, though Doug's spirits appeared to have sunk into his shoes. 'I came in a taxi so I didn't have to worry about driving under the influence. With a bit of luck he'll still be waiting. I paid him enough to hang about.'

Holly looked at him with a softened smile. She had been wrong.

Joel had had every intention of going to the party, after all.

Unless, of course, it was all part and parcel of his little game to win her over.

10

The party was already under way when they arrived and there were a few curious and disbelieving stares when Holly walked in with Doug on one side of her, and Joel on the other.

Kay was the first to single out Holly as soon as she got separated from her two male escorts.

'Holly! We all thought you weren't coming.'

'Well, I changed my mind.'

She scoured the room and picked out Joel talking to Charles Smith — Uncle Charles, that was — down by the buffet table.

Doug was sitting morosely near the deafening hi-fi unit as it played disco music from the Seventies and there was a girl from Accounts trying to engage him in a discussion on something or other and not having much success.

'It's a great party,' Kay told Holly and she noticed that her friend was just a little unsteady on her feet.

Holly was even more grateful for the two glasses of champagne inside her that would, she was sure, see her to the end of the evening.

'Excuse me, Kay.' Holly started walking away. 'I see Santa Claus over there and I have a few words to say to him.'

'You go ahead, sweetie!' Kay waved her off.

Joel and his uncle were deep in some kind of intimate discussion with their backs to the room when Holly finally reached them, having been stopped by various colleagues on the way.

'You didn't tell her anything, did you?' she heard Charles say in his rather deep, gravely voice. 'I can't have this thing being leaked out.'

'She doesn't know anything for sure, but she's obviously suspicious,' Joel hissed back.

'Blast!' The grizzly Santa, tonight looking very smart in civvies, helped himself to some more punch and grimaced as he swallowed a mouthful. 'God awful stuff this!'

'Is everything still organised for tomorrow?'

'Yes. I'm sure none of them cottoned on. I was very careful the way I got their addresses out of them.'

'Well, look at this!' Holly slapped them both on the back and they jumped a mile, both spilling their drinks. 'You look like Buffalo Bill and the Cincinnati Kid. Or is it Starsky and Hutch? Or Bonnie and Clyde?'

She saw Joel frowning down at her from beneath his winged brows.

'Would one of you fine gentlemen please tell me what it is you are up to, so I can maybe inform the police?'

'Holly, stop this,' Joel said softly, putting a hand on her shoulder, which she immediately brushed off.

'Will you tell me, Joel?' she persisted. 'Or will you — Uncle Charles? Uncle Charles Richards, I believe it is, am I not correct?'

They stared at her, then exchanged anxious looks.

'I'm rumbled,' Charles Richards said and ran a trembling hand over his beard, which had yet to return to its normal steely grey.

'Holly, I can explain — everything,' Joel said and it sounded like he was reading from a cheap film script. 'But how did you find out about — about us?'

'That he's your uncle and . . . ' Holly drew in a breath and let it out in a long, exasperated sigh. 'And the owner of The Playpen chain of stores. A millionaire, no less, and he did a penniless old man out of a much-needed job just so he could play at being Santa Claus. What kind of excuse can you give for that, eh?'

'Barnstable was paid very well not to do the job,' Joel said.

'He never did it for the money!'

'And neither did I, my dear,' Charles said and Holly noticed that his eyes had become misty. 'Joel, she'll have to come in on our little subterfuge. Will you tell her, please? I'm feeling rather tired. I think I'll go home so I'm fresh for tomorrow.'

Joel nodded and they watched the old man walk, stiff-backed and proud, through the milling crowd of staff and their guests.

Of course, everybody knew him by now and he got many pats on the back and shouts of, 'Merry Christmas, Santa!' as he wended his way through them to the exit.

In whichever disguise she saw him, be it Charles Smith, Charles Richards or Santa Claus, Holly could not fully bring herself to see him as a criminal. And yet, what else could he possibly be involved in, but crime?

11

'But why can't you tell me here and now?' Holly demanded as Joel almost manhandled her out of the hotel and into a taxi. 'You might have let me say good-night to Doug before kidnapping me,' she added scathingly as she sat in the back passenger seat and Joel climbed in beside her, giving the driver her address. 'What's he going to think?'

'I don't much care what he thinks.'

'Have you or your uncle ever had to work for anything in your rich, millionaire lives?' Holly felt it was better to change the subject.

She saw him smile through the dimness of the taxicab and heard a low, throaty laugh.

'My uncle might be a millionaire, Holly, but I most certainly am not. And yes, I have had to work — and work jolly hard. Uncle Charles wasn't always rich. He was raised in the back streets of London and his parents didn't even have the price of shoe-leather, so he went to school in his bare feet. But he never let poverty stop him from learning and he taught me everything I know, by making me start at the bottom.'

'You expect me to believe that?'

'Look me up in Miss Loach's personnel records, if you don't believe me. At eighteen I was sweeping floors and stacking shelves at the London branch and nobody knew who I was so I wouldn't get preferential treatment.'

Holly shook her head.

'I've already looked for your records, Joel. The file exists, but it's empty.'

'Then Miss Loach must have removed the papers for security purposes.' Holly groaned at that.

'Oh, Joel! You've done nothing but lie, cheat and prevaricate from the minute you arrived here in Newcastle. No wonder I can't believe you now.'

They fell silent. Holly sat, huddled in

her red dress, under her sheepskin coat and watched the silvery white landscape go by.

She listened to the creaky crunch of the car tyres in the fresh snow and wished there was such a person as a Fairy Godmother with a magic wand and she was Cinderella and Joel . . . No! Joel could never be her Prince Charming, she decided. He was too dishonest by far.

Again, he asked the cab driver to wait outside Holly's block of flats.

They went up, their footsteps echoing hollowly on the stairs. She got out her door key and turned to face Joel.

'Right, you can tell me now just exactly what you're up to, then I'd like you to leave.'

'And what if I don't want to leave?'

'Do you think you have a choice?'

'There's always a choice, Holly.'

He took her quite by surprise, coming forward like that, pressing her back against the door and, with his hand tilting up her face, he kissed her long and hard so that when he eventually lifted his head, her lips felt bruised and tingling. In fact, her whole being was tingling and she was ashamed at the kind of effect his kiss had had on her.

'Please, Joel — don't do this to me. Don't play with me as if I were worth nothing.'

'Actually, Holly, you may not realise it, but you're worth a fortune to me.'

⋆   ⋆   ⋆

Holly felt herself go all limp as if her bones were beginning to melt inside her. She knew she mustn't weaken so far that she would not be able to resist him, but the darker side of her personality was yearning for him to take her in his arms again, kiss her and belong totally to her.

'You're a married man, Joel. I'm not prepared to get involved, so don't even contemplate it.'

He shook his head, closed his eyes,

then opened them again and stroked Holly's face gently, beautifully.

How he had taken the key from her paralysed hand, she would never know, but he was fitting it into the lock, opening the door and pushing her inside.

'Just tell me about Charles Smith — I mean, Richards — and then — please go!'

'Yes, I'll tell you about him, Holly, but first, let me tell you a little more about myself.'

Maybe it was the champagne working inside her still, but Holly let him lead her to the sofa, take off her coat and sling it over the back of a chair. Then they were sitting close and he was holding one of her hands in both of his, one thumb stroking the inside of her wrist.

★   ★   ★

'First of all, I'm not married,' he said. 'I'm divorced. Cheryl is my ex-wife. You

115

spoke to her on the phone . . . ' His mouth lifted at one side in a wry smile and she coloured at the memory of that short conversation.

'She and my daughter live with my parents in London. Or they did until the day I was due to visit. They are now in Australia with Cheryl's new partner.

'I've spoken to Kelly and she thinks Australia's great. She's eight years old and although I see her when I can, it hadn't really been enough to cement a good father/daughter relationship. Like her mother, she's also crazy about her new stepfather. It was that whole situation that drove me to come up here to the north-east. So, you see . . . '

He spread his hands and looked at Holly plaintively. She wrinkled her nose and chewed reflectively on her mouth.

'So you're not married. OK. But why all the mystery surrounding you and your uncle?'

He rubbed his forehead and the smile faded fast from his face.

'That's more difficult for me to

explain,' he said, reaching in his pocket for his mobile phone, which had chosen that moment to bleep.

Holly moved into the kitchen with the intention of making some strong black coffee, but he was suddenly there with her, his face grey with worry.

'What is it?'

She fully expected him to tell her that he had to leave in a hurry because the police were on to him and his uncle, but she was only half correct.

'It was the hospital. My uncle's house has been burgled. He arrived home and caught them at it.'

'You said the hospital,' Holly reminded him curiously.

'One of the burglars hit him and he fell down the stairs trying to chase them off the premises.'

'Oh, no!'

Her concern for the old man, whoever, whatever, was totally genuine. She had been trying not to like him, but had failed — just as she had failed miserably in her dislike of his nephew.

'Is he badly hurt?'

'A mild concussion, they said.' Joel was already heading for the door. 'And a sprained ankle.'

'Poor soul! But at least it's not life-threatening.'

Joel was at the door and he turned and fixed her with a withering look.

'You don't understand, Holly. It's actually far more serious than you could possibly imagine.'

'You're right,' Holly said. 'I don't understand. You still haven't told me what kind of shady business you and your uncle are up to.'

'Nothing criminal, I can assure you.' He hesitated, running a hand over his thick hair as she had seen him do so many times when he wasn't sure of something. 'Look, Holly, get your coat. I hope to goodness that taxi's still waiting, because we'll never get another one at this time of night on Christmas Eve.'

'You want me to go with you? Where?'

'To the hospital, of course!' He had spoken sharply, then thought better of it and gave her a small smile of exasperation mingled with apology. 'I'm sorry. It's just that so much hung on everything going right tonight and now . . .'

'And now?'

'It's all gone terribly wrong. Would you please come with me to the hospital to see my uncle, Holly? I'll explain everything to you on the way and I hope you'll want to help when you hear the truth.'

'The truth?' She didn't know whether to feel angry or pleased. 'Do you mean the truth as in what you've been telling me up to now, Joel — or the truth as it really is?'

'You'll have to judge that for yourself.'

★   ★   ★

By the time they reached the hospital, Holly knew it all. It was a crazy, crazy

119

story. Perhaps too crazy not to be true.

She started by not believing a word, then, when she thought more deeply about what Joel was telling her and how much she already knew, Holly could see that she was going to have to trust him. And trust his uncle at the same time.

An officious-looking staff nurse grudgingly told them that Charles Richards was as well as could be expected under the circumstances and was, much against doctor's advice, waiting to see them.

'He's just finished talking to the police,' the nurse told them as she led them to the private cubicle at the edge of the big, general ward. 'He's exhausted, but he wouldn't settle until I agreed to telephone you.'

'That was very kind of you,' Joel said with his usual charm and Holly could see the woman's icy edges beginning to melt, though she still regarded Holly frostily.

'You can have five minutes, but he is sedated, so don't be surprised if he falls asleep while you're talking.'

'We'll be as quick as we can, Nurse, thank you.'

Charles Richards looked pale and weak and much older lying in his hospital bed.

His iron-grey head nestled in the deep pillows. His blue-veined hands lay motionless on the counterpane. His eyes were closed, but as Holly and Joel entered the cubicle the lids fluttered and opened and he gave them a bright, blue stare.

'You're here at last!' One hand came up, reaching towards Joel, who came forward and clasped it.

'Uncle Charles! What on earth happened?'

The old man blinked up at him, then noticed Holly's presence for the first time and smiled wearily in her direction.

There was a large bruise spreading on one side of his forehead and he had the makings of a black eye. Nothing serious, she thought, but he looked so fragile lying there.

'Does she know yet?' Charles Richards asked, his voice as thin as tissue paper.

'Yes.' Joel nodded. 'And she's agreed to help us, but what about these burglars?'

'Don't worry about them,' his uncle said. 'I was able to give good descriptions to the police and the young constable who took my statement said he recognised one of them. A local gang, apparently. I figure they'll have them behind bars before long.'

'Holly thought that you and I were part of the gang,' Joel said, turning and grinning at her over his shoulder and she blushed.

'So that's why you were a bit tetchy, young lady! Well, I never.'

'You have to admit the pair of you have been acting very suspiciously,' Holly said with a frown.

A tired chuckle escaped the old man's lips.

'And now that you know what we're

really up to, how does that make you feel?'

Holly drew in a deep breath.

'Scared,' she said and meant it.

'Not half as scared as I have been lately, my dear,' Charles said with a quick glance in Joel's direction. 'Joel here has been a tower of strength, despite problems of his own.'

'Yes, well, let's not dwell on my problems,' Joel said wistfully.

'I trust you've got them all sorted now, my boy?'

Joel nodded and his eyes flicked over Holly's face.

'As well as possible,' he said.

'And a good thing, too. Now, you must start a new life — reinvent yourself. Isn't that what they say today? Strange expression, but I'm sure you young people know what it means.'

The old man drew in a deep breath and let out a long, shuddering sigh, then seeing the anxiety in Holly's eyes, he reached out and squeezed her hand, smiling wearily.

'I'm all right, child. Now, before this sedative carries me off into the arms of Morpheus, can we talk of more urgent matters? We are running out of time fast.'

12

'Still scared, Holly?' Holly looked up at Joel and, heaving a sigh, started to nod, then changed her mind and shook her head.

'Oh, I don't know, Joel,' she told him. 'I don't think scared is actually the right word, but I do still think it's crazy — crazy and really rather wonderful, what you and your uncle are doing.'

They were back in the taxi again and the driver, having been given a cup of hot hospital tea, was looking warmer and getting to be one of the team with his brash smile and gruff voice.

'Where to now, guv?' he wanted to know.

Joel took Holly's hand and squeezed it and she wished he hadn't, because it stirred feelings inside her that she knew were a waste of time.

'The Playpen on Northumberland

Street,' he said to the driver, not taking his eyes off her. 'Do you know it?'

The driver grinned even more broadly.

'Know it? My wife says, 'Ted,' she says to me, 'it's like kiddie's heaven in that place.' My lad practically lives there and the missus spends so much there every Christmas she should own shares in the profits.'

'Well, that could be arranged, Ted, if you would give us a helping hand tonight.'

The cab driver looked wary. He glanced Holly's way, then his eyes turned questioningly back to Joel.

'What kind of helping hand, mate?' he wanted to know.

'Nothing you'll regret,' Joel said. 'Ever fancy being one of Santa Claus's helpers? That's virtually what Holly and I are tonight, eh, Holly?'

She smiled and nodded. In her mind she could still see poor old Charles Richards lying there in his hospital bed, fighting valiantly against pain and the effects of a strong sedative, in order to tell them what he expected of them.

It was a tall order and one Holly didn't know they could carry out by the deadline, even with the help of a third party.

Deadline. The word carried Holly's thoughts along a very different route. That of Charles Richards' life. A self-made man, an unqualified success in business — and a total failure at being happy.

Those were his words. He had beckoned her forward, indicating that she should sit on the edge of his bed.

And, as she sat there, he recounted how he had pushed himself to the maximum, honestly believing that his success as a businessman was the ultimate reward and that he would want nothing else.

He had never married, never known what it was like to raise a child, be a part of a normal, happy, family unit.

All his life he had been shy of women, scared of commitment. All his life, he had been lonely.

Then, at the age of seventy, he had been diagnosed with cancer.

A few months, the doctors had given him, at most a year, maybe. Suddenly he saw himself as a failure.

He had built up an empire, a chain of toy stores that were unique and offered everybody, every child, a chance of happiness . . .

That is, every child with parents who could afford to buy toys sold by The Playpen. What of the poor people, he had wondered one day on seeing a child die before his eyes in the cancer clinic.

What about mothers, fathers, who did not have enough money to buy expensive presents? Parents who struggled from one year's end to the next crying silently because their children were being deprived.

That was when the idea came to him. He would, in the time he had left, become a kind of godfather to as many poor, deprived children as he could find. And he could find them by donning the robe of Santa Claus, the greatest godfather of all time.

But he could not bear the idea of anyone knowing who he was or what he was doing — and especially why he was doing it. He didn't want their pity. Nor did he want their derision.

Joel, who had been the closest member of the family to Charles, was the only person to be taken into his confidence.

By moving Joel into the newly-vacated branch manager's position in Newcastle, he was able to secure the job of Santa Claus without too many embarrassing questions being asked. And it helped Joel, too, because his marital situation was getting to be more and more of a problem.

★   ★   ★

'So there you are, my dear,' the old man had said, his eyelids drooping as he fought off sleep. 'Now you know our little secret. But these thugs, these burglars, have ruined it all for me. Maybe I wasn't meant to make up for my miserable life by doing good. I'm going to die the way I lived, in the greatest poverty of all. Rich, miserable and alone.'

His voice was fading and his eyes were now shut. Holly leaned forward and kissed him gently on the cheek.

He stirred and his pale lips curled into a smile. She felt Joel's hand heavy on her shoulder, telling her they should be going.

'Can we really make this thing work?' Holly asked him as they left the cubicle with a swift, backward glance at the sleeping man. 'We can't let him die without helping him to realise his last dream.'

'No, but we may not have a choice,' Joel said with a frown. 'I'm not sure we can pull it off in time.'

His idea had left Holly breathless, but she was game to go along with it. After all, what else did she have to do that Christmas Eve?

13

Charles Richards had carefully gathered as many addresses as he could from genuinely poor families among the hordes of children who had visited Santa's Grotto.

At Christmas it was the store's policy to put on a Santa Claus who was free for all, so parents with little money could at least visit, even if they couldn't afford to buy. And a small, inexpensive gift was always given, free of charge, to every child.

As the list and the Christmas wishes grew, Charles had obtained major presents for all and stored them in his great big, lonely mansion.

The families on his list had been sent invitations to spend Christmas Day with him. Now, thanks to the burglars, most of the gifts had vanished. Joel's and Holly's task was to get them back, by hook or by crook.

They were extremely lucky in a way, since most of the items had been chosen from the shelves of The Playpen. Assuming the stock was not exhausted, they could replace the things without too much bother, but time wasn't exactly on their side.

'We'll never make it!' Holly said breathlessly as they rushed around the silent shop floor, piling everything near the front entrance door.

'Maybe not, but I'm determined to try,' Joel said, patting Ted on the back as the driver passed by carrying a huge stuffed panda. 'Good man, Ted.'

'We'll never do it, guv!' Ted said, turning and speaking over the panda's head. 'Not without more help. This lot's got to be transported and wrapped and . . . '

'Any suggestions?'

'Aye, I have. Why don't we get all the lads in on this?'

'I'm not sure that . . . '

Holly tugged at Joel's arm.

'Just a minute, Joel. Let's hear what

Ted has to say. Go on, Ted.' Ted scratched his balding head and twisted his mouth.

'There's a bunch of us drivers not working tonight. Bit of a protest against having to drive drunkards around.

'Anyhow,' Ted continued, 'I know where I can get my hands on them — the lads, that is. If you like, I'll enlist them. They're a good bunch.'

'Well . . . ' Joel scratched the back of his neck and glanced at Holly. 'I know my uncle didn't want anybody to know about all this, but . . . '

'We'll never manage without help,' she told him and he nodded.

'OK, Ted. Get on to your men and ask them to assemble here, but don't push too hard, eh? I want willing volunteers, not men who feel they're being press-ganged.'

'You leave it to me, guv!'

And they did leave it to Ted and he came through for them.

Within half an hour there was a troop of taxis lining up and a string of drivers carrying toys out into the street.

Then the police arrived.

⋆   ⋆   ⋆

Holly had never been inside a police station before, though it was exactly as she imagined it might be.

It was a square box of magnolia-painted walls, no-nonsense desks and chairs, stiff uniformed policemen and the ubiquitous through-put of drunks, belligerent bar-room brawlers and other people who had entered into the Christmas spirit a bit too readily.

The thing that made it all somehow surreal was the fact that there were Christmas streamers strung across the ceiling and carols playing softly in the background. It was difficult to take any of it seriously.

'Right then!'

The desk sergeant was a large barrel of a man with a florid complexion and a bristling moustache. 'What 'ave we 'ere, then?'

The two arresting officers also stepped forward, notebooks at the ready. Behind her, Holly could feel the press of taxi drivers, hot and steamy from their exertions and, perhaps, their fear of having their licences revoked.

'I can explain,' she heard Joel say, when another large policeman in plain clothes sauntered nonchalantly through from some back room, a cup of tea in his hand.

'What's this all about, Sergeant?'

The sergeant turned quickly and fingered his tight collar.

'I was just about to find out, sir. The lads brought this lot in, saying something about a break-in on Northumberland Street. A toy shop, by all accounts.'

'The Playpen,' Joel supplied and turned to the senior of the two policemen. 'If I could be allowed to explain the situation?'

That was when Ted, their stalwart taxi-driver friend, stepped forward and intervened on their behalf.

'Before you think of locking us all up, Superintendent Lockhart, I just want to tell you that this whole thing is innocent. This man is helping out Santa Claus — he's his nephew — and there are a lot of children who are going to be disappointed come tomorrow. We were just giving him a helping hand, like.'

'I'm sure you were.' Dark, sceptical brows shot up, then, 'Ah, it's Ted Burrows, isn't it? How are you doing, Ted? Wife and kids all right?'

Ted coloured up and grinned.

'Aye, sir. They're grand, but . . . '

'So why aren't you at home with them tonight? Good Lord, man, it's Christmas Eve.'

'I could ask the same of you, sir,' Ted said, unabashed.

'That's different. I'm a policeman. Crime never takes a holiday and nor do we. Just like the doctors over in the infirmary. You can't tell people not to get sick just because it's Christmas.'

Holly could see Joel getting impatient, shuffling from one foot to the

136

other. The superintendent saw it, too, and gave a short, curious laugh.

'Ted and I are old friends,' he explained. 'He delivered my first child a few years ago.'

Ted laughed, too.

'Aye. The little blighter wouldn't wait till we got his mother to hospital. How is young Edward, sir?'

'He's doing fine, thanks to you. Now, who's going to tell me what's going on here?'

★   ★   ★

There were cheers all round when they were informed, a few minutes later, that they were free to go.

Not only that, the superintendent had loaned them one or two of his uniformed lads to help make up for lost time.

They needed all the help they could get. It was now a question of rushing around to the shop-owners. Holly had telephoned earlier, tracking down the items they still lacked.

At first she had been met by a few disgruntled responses, but in the end they all came through when they knew what they were dealing with.

Nobody lost out, apart from an hour or two of sleep. As for Holly and Joel, they had too much adrenalin flowing to allow them to feel tired.

All the presents were transported as swiftly as possible to Charles Richards' home.

The volunteers set to wrapping and labelling every one of them, hoping they didn't make any mistakes and mix up fire engines with cuddly dolls.

It was five in the morning when they said their grateful goodbyes to the taxi drivers and the lads in blue.

As the door closed on the last one to leave, Holly felt exhaustion kicking in.

'Tired?' Joel asked softly as she sagged against the doorjamb and stifled a yawn.

'That's understating it a bit,' she told him with a weak smile. 'I'd better get back home before I become comatose.'

'Stay here,' he said and Holly looked at him sideways, not quite understanding the undertone in his voice.

He gave a weary grin.

'We have plenty of guest rooms. Don't worry, Holly. I don't have any designs on you. Not tonight, anyway. I'm far too tired.'

Holly wasn't sure quite how to take the, not tonight anyway, but thought it was probably all quite innocent.

Besides, Joel was looking so introspective and sad she didn't think he was in the mood to take advantage of anybody just then.

'I don't know . . . '

'Come on.' He gripped her hand and drew her after him across the hall and up the grand staircase to the first floor. 'I'm in no state to drive and you'll never find a taxi now.'

He was right, of course.

Holly could have walked and got to her flat in about four hours — ridiculous thought. She could hear the wind buffeting the house, whistling through cracks and down chimneys. And the snow was still falling thick and fast. They would be lucky not to get snowed in.

'I think you'll find everything you need in here,' Joel said, throwing open one of the doors on a long corridor of guest rooms. 'My sister used to come here in the holidays. You'll find some of her things still here. She has no further use for them, since she and her husband moved to Florida, so don't worry about it.'

'Oh! I'm not sure that I should . . . '

'Don't be silly, Holly. Who's it going to hurt?'

Holly wasn't sure about that.

'Well, I don't know exactly . . . '

'They're not my ex-wife's if that's what you're thinking. Not that it would matter. I got over my divorce a long time ago. There's nothing left of the marriage to hurt me — all except, perhaps . . . '

His voice trailed off and she saw a

melancholy creeping into his eyes.

'Your little girl?'

He shrugged.

'It's Christmas!' he said with a crack in his voice.

'There'll be other Christmases,' Holly said and he smiled and nodded. 'In the meantime, you have an awful lot of children to make happy tomorrow. You'd better get some sleep, too.'

Holly heard him wandering about downstairs long after she had sunk into the big, double bed and turned out the light, but eventually even he stopped his wanderings and settled down.

All was silent and peaceful, except for the soughing of the wind.

14

Holly awoke to the muted sounds of a radio playing Christmas hymns, someone whistling softly along, and the mouth-watering smell of bacon, toast and coffee.

As quickly as she could she showered and climbed back into her red dress that, mercifully, wasn't too creased from the night before. Then she followed her nose to the kitchen.

Joel was sitting at a big scrubbed pine table in the centre of the old-fashioned room, a large glass of fresh orange juice in his hand. Bacon was sizzling in a pan on the ancient Aga cooker and a coffee percolator was making lascivious noises to itself in the far corner.

'Well timed!' Joel said, standing up and pulling out a chair.

'I didn't have an alarm,' Holly said apologetically, painfully aware that her face was almost totally without make-up since she had only a lipstick with her, though she had borrowed a flick or two of his sister's mascara which she found in the dressing-table drawer. 'I'm afraid I slept like a log.'

'Me, too. Come on, eat up, then we've got to get ready.'

Both their heads swung around as the telephone shrilled loudly. Joel went to it and she saw him listening intently as she made a start on the bacon and eggs he had placed before her.

'Well, that was good news!' he said, coming back to the table. 'It was the police to say they've caught the villain who broke in here — and recovered all the stolen goods, ours as well as a whole warehouse full of other things that had been destined as Christmas presents.'

Although heartened by the news, Holly gave a groan.

'So, all our efforts were in vain last night!'

Joel gave a tired smile.

'Oh, I wouldn't say that. I got a lot out of it. I made a few new friends, became a better person — I hope — and . . . '

'And?'

'I got to know you a lot better.'

'And that's good, is it?' Holly asked the question while inwardly her insides tensed.

He nodded.

'I would say it was very good. You're not such a stiff and starchy person after all, are you, Holly? You worked your fingers to the bone last night so those poor kids could have a nice Christmas. I'd call that pretty special, wouldn't you?'

'If you say so.'

'I do. Now, if you're finished eating . . . '

★   ★   ★

The house was positively throbbing with excitement. Children and their parents had been transported from far and wide and Charles's housekeeper, Mrs Robinson, had arrived with a team of helpers and a mouth-watering festive feast that was just waiting to be served.

'Holly!'

She heard the shout from across the spacious drawing-room and saw a hand waving above the heads of the milling crowd of children. Then a face bobbed up and down and she recognised little Harry as he barged his way through, dragging a gaggle of dumbfounded brothers and sisters with him.

'Harry! Oh, I'm so pleased to see you.' Holly bent down and gave him a hug, then turned her attention to the others. 'So this is your family?'

'Aye! And me mam's here an' all,' he told her excitedly. 'She's — aw, come on, Mam! She's scared you'll tell her off for pinching stuff in your shop.'

Holly scanned the crowd and saw the painfully thin woman with the sad face whom she had seen previously when Harry had been detained by Kay. Their eyes met. Holly smiled and saw the woman's mouth twitch uncertainly at the corners as she made her way towards her family.

'Hello!' Holly held out her hand and Harry's mother shook it briefly, looking awkward. 'I'm sorry. I don't know your name.'

'It's Johnson! Ellen Johnson.'

'Ellen will do. I'm Holly. Harry and I are old friends. I'm so glad you could all come here today.'

The woman seemed very emotional and almost on the verge of tears. Holly guessed what kind of Christmas they would have had, were it not for a certain very kind old man.

The thought of Charles Richards, lying hurt and sick in his hospital bed, brought a lump to her throat and a tightness to her heart that she found difficult to suppress. Charles's dream was happening all around her and the man himself, who had made it all possible, couldn't be there to see it.

Joel touched her elbow.

'Holly, we'd better get things started. Mrs Robinson is agitating to start on the food before it spoils.'

'What are we going to do?' she asked, looking around her at the expectant faces and knowing exactly what was going through their minds. 'We don't have a Santa Claus.'

He blew out his cheeks and rubbed the back of his neck. 'We'll just have to spin them some sort of tale about Santa having an accident or something. After all, it's only half a lie.'

'Couldn't you do it?' She gazed up at him, then grinned at the absurdity of the thought. 'No, I suppose it would look a bit odd, you being so much taller than your uncle. The outfit would never fit.'

He grinned back at her. 'Oh, well, here goes!'

He clapped his hands twice and called for silence. Everybody stopped talking and looked in his direction.

'As you know, children, Santa was

supposed to be with us today to give out the presents you all wished for, but . . . '

There was a uniform exclamation all around and she saw Joel flinch. They hadn't known about the presents. It was supposed to be a surprise. He flashed a look at Holly and was about to continue when a rush of cold air made everybody gasp and shiver.

There was a silvery tinkle of garden chimes and a flurry of glistening snowflakes floated in, together with a red-clad figure, limping on a crutch, but ho-ho-ing and ha-ha-ing in good old traditional style.

'Good Lord!' Joel whispered in Holly's ear. 'It's Uncle Charles!'

'And I didn't believe in miracles!'

She laughed back at him and almost cried when he reached out and clutched her hand. Then, raising it to his lips, he kissed the backs of her fingers in such a way she wanted to tell him to stop, only it felt so good she couldn't bear to utter a word.

'I do — now,' he said softly, though she could hardly hear him above the din that was exploding right through the house. 'But I also know that miracles don't just happen. They sometimes need an awful lot of help. Thank you, Holly, for yours.'

Their short, tubby Santa Claus was incredible. Not one child was missed out and every parent got a gift, too. There were a lot of damp eyes and quivering lips in the midst of tearing paper and discarded boxes, which Joel and Holly cleared away as Mrs Robinson tapped an impatient foot and reminded them about her turkeys going dry in the kitchen.

With the help of the parents, every available space was cleared and laid out with trestle tables, on which there were Christmas crackers, paper hats and games to keep everybody busy between courses.

Joel and Holly sat on either side of Charles Richards and Holly couldn't help thinking how well the old man looked, despite his traumatic experience. Here, indeed, was one happy man, having realised his dream and done something good for his fellow human beings less fortunate than he was.

'How are you feeling, Uncle Charles?' Joel asked, his hand resting anxiously on the old man's arm.

'Never felt better!' Charles Richards shook his bearded head and laughed. It was the most jovial sound Holly had ever heard. 'And you know what? I've had a reprieve.'

'A what?' Joel's brows knitted together, and he glanced over at Holly.

Charles was still chuckling into his beard and Holly wondered if he was on some happy drug or had been tippling at the whisky too freely.

'A reprieve, laddie! While I was in hospital, my oncologist came to see me and do you know what?'

'What?' Both Joel and Holly answered simultaneously.

'They say the cancer's in remission.

They don't know how it's happened, but there you are! I hope when the end comes it will be because of real old age and not some illness.'

They almost suffocated the poor man with their hugs and cries of delight, which raised a few curious eyebrows, but neither of them cared and it was obvious that Joel's uncle didn't either.

15

'So,' Joel said later as he and Holly walked out together into the navy blue of the evening with its carpet of virgin snow. 'Miracles do happen after all.'

'Yes,' she said, aware that he was hugging her arm tightly to his side as they walked, making tracks and breathing out clouds of freezing vapour. 'I suppose they do.'

Holly was thinking that the only miracle she would like to see happen right then was the impossible one.

At least, it wouldn't happen for her. It would happen to some lucky girl who looked right and came from the right background and walked into Joel's life at the right time.

'I don't suppose,' he said, halting and turning her to face him, 'that you would care to make just one more person happy on this Christmas Day?'

She stared at him, silently for a while, blocking out any thought that dared enter into her fanciful mind.

'Who's that then?'

'You're looking at him.'

Holly gave an audible gasp as his arms snaked around her.

His face came close, oh, so close. She started to push him away, then saw the hurt in his dark eyes.

'I don't understand, Joel,' she told him hesitantly.

He gave a slight laugh.

'Neither do I, Holly, but one way or another I feel the need to prove something to you.'

'Oh?'

He nodded.

'I thought I would never fall in love again, thought there wasn't a woman in this world that could make me feel — well, the way I'm feeling right now.'

'Oh?' It was such a small, pathetic sound, but Holly couldn't trust herself to say more.

'That's how you feel, too, isn't it,

Holly? I'm not wrong, am I?'

'No.' She croaked out that one word and her knees started to melt as he kissed her, gently at first, then with a hungry passion that warmed her all the way through.

Up above them the stars were lighting up and twinkling merrily. You could almost imagine the sleigh and the reindeer and the jolly old man in the red suit soaring high into the galaxy with a jingle of bells and a jolly ho-ho-ho.

Framed in the big bay window of the drawing-room, their real-life Santa Claus was regarding them, nodding, smiling and applauding silently. They laughed and waved to him and Holly felt suddenly warm and loved and wanted. No season had ever been so full of goodwill.

Now, at last, she had the impossible miracle she had prayed for. And already she felt part of a new and happy family.